Further Tales of Uncle Remus

THE MISADVENTURES OF BRER RABBIT, BRER FOX, BRER WOLF, THE DOODANG, AND OTHER CREATURES

Further Tales of Uncle Remus

The Misadventures of Brer Rabbit, Brer Fox,
Brer Wolf, the Doodang, and Other Creatures

as told by JULIUS LESTER

illustrated by Jerry Pinkney

DIAL BOOKS

New York

Published by Dial Books
A Division of Penguin Books USA Inc.
375 Hudson Street
New York, New York 10014
Published simultaneously in Canada by
Fitzhenry & Whiteside Limited, Toronto
Text copyright © 1990 by Julius Lester
Illustrations copyright © 1990 by Jerry Pinkney
All rights reserved
Design by Jane Byers Bierhorst
Printed in the U.S.A.
First Edition
W
10 9 8 7 6 5 4 3 2 1

Library of Congress Cataloging in Publication Data

Lester, Julius.
Further tales of Uncle Remus. The misadventures of
Brer Rabbit, Brer Fox, Brer Wolf, the Doodang,
and other creatures.

Summary: A retelling of the classic Afro-American tales
relating the adventures and misadventures of
Brer Rabbit and his friends and enemies.
1. Afro-Americans—Folklore.   2. Tales—United States.
[1. Folklore, Afro-American.   2. Animals—Folklore.]
I. Pinkney, Jerry, ill.   II. Title.   III. Title: Further
Adventures of Uncle Remus.   IV. Title: Misadventures of
Brer Rabbit, Brer Fox, Brer Wolf, the Doodang, and other creatures.
PZ8.1.L434Fu 1990   398.2′08996073   88-20223
ISBN 0-8037-0610-3   ISBN 0-8037-0611-1 (lib. bdg.)

The publisher wishes to express its sincere thanks to the estate
of Joel Chandler Harris for its gracious support during the
publication of this new version of The Tales of Uncle Remus.

Each black-and-white drawing is made of pencil and graphite; and
each full-color picture consists of a pencil, graphite, and watercolor
painting that is color-separated and reproduced in full color.

Contents

Further Tales of Uncle Remus

THE MISADVENTURES OF BRER RABBIT, BRER FOX, BRER WOLF, THE DOODANG, AND OTHER CREATURES

Brer Fox and Mr. Man

Many evenings I'll be sitting here thinking about much of nothing and the door will open a crack. I know who it is, so I don't get scared. Instead I close my eyes partways and pretend like I'm napping. After a minute or two I'll see two long ears come around the door followed by two of the biggest eyeballs you've ever seen. I'll give out with a loud snore like I'm sleeping as sound as the Man in the Moon.

Brer Rabbit will look at me real hard, and once he's convinced that I'm asleep, he'll beckon to the other creatures—Brer Fox, Brer Wolf, Brer Turtle, Mr. Benjamin Ram, and all the rest of them—and they'll come in real quiet, pull up chairs, and sit right there in front of the fireplace.

Mr. Benjamin Ram will take out his fiddle and start playing one of them old-time tunes what's been marinated in hard times and high hopes, and them creatures will get to singing and dancing and having a good time. When they're out of breath, they'll go back there in the kitchen and pop some popcorn and make some Kool-Aid and come back in here, and then they'll get to remembering the old times. Brer Fox will remind Brer Rabbit of some trick or other. Then Brer Wolf will remember something else and Brer Turtle will remember his remembrances. When all the popcorn and Kool-Aid is gone, and they've laughed themselves almost into the hospital, they'll wash and dry all the bowls and glasses and everything and go out just as quiet as they come in. I'll open my eyes then and laugh and laugh and laugh about all the things them creatures used to do.

Like Brer Fox, for example. Some folks say Brer Fox was no 'count and good for nothing. Others say he was a schemer and a conniver, and them was his good qualities! Of all the things I heard folks say about him, though, I never did hear nobody say Brer Fox was smart.

One morning Brer Fox was going through the woods when he heard a wagon coming along the road. He hid behind a tree. In a few minutes here come Mr. Man in his wagon, which was loaded down with eggs and butter and chickens. He was on his way to market.

If Brer Fox had his way, Mr. Man might get to market but not with his eggs, butter, and chickens. He was sorry Brer Rabbit wasn't around, because Brer Rabbit would've found a way to get the eggs, butter, and chicken and Mr. Man's horse and wagon too. But Brer Rabbit had won the lottery and was off scuba diving in Jamaica.

Thinking of Brer Rabbit reminded him of the time he went hunting and on his way home with a big bag of game, he came across a dead rabbit lying in the road. About a half mile farther along there was another one. A quarter mile after that he came across still another one. Not being a man to turn down a gift from the Lord, Brer Fox had put down his game bag and gone back to get the rabbits. But when he got back to the place where the first rabbit had been, it wasn't there. What he had thought was a dead rabbit wasn't nothing but Brer Rabbit pretending to be dead. Brer Fox was looking for rabbits what didn't exist, and Brer Rabbit was making off with his game bag.

That was a good trick, and Brer Fox figured that since it had worked on him, it would work on Mr. Man. That tells you right there that Brer Fox's elevator didn't go all the way to the top.

Brer Fox ran through the woods until he got a ways in front of Mr. Man, and he lay down in the road like he was dead. A few minutes later Mr. Man come along, singing to himself. I don't know what he was singing. It was probably the blues, 'cause when a body is feeling good, they got to sing the blues. Then again, when a body is feeling bad they got to sing the blues. Just goes to show how powerful the blues is. No matter how you feeling, singing the blues'll make you feel better.

So Mr. Man is sitting there in his wagon singing the

blues, and all of a sudden his horse whinnied and reared up. Mr. Man took his mind off the blues and put it on the horse and he hollered, "Whoa!" and the horse whoa'd.

Mr. Man saw Brer Fox laying on the ground looking as dead as a New Year's resolution on January second.

Mr. Man laughed. "Well, well, well. There's the one what's been stealing my chickens. Looks like somebody shot him with a gun. Too bad they didn't use two guns."

Mr. Man told the horse to "Giddup," drove around Brer Fox, and went on his way.

Brer Fox got up, ran through the woods until he was a ways in front of Mr. Man, and lay down in the road again.

A few minutes later here come Mr. Man. Mr. Man told his horse to "Whoa!" and the horse whoa'd. "Well, well, well. There's the one what's been stealing my pigs. Looks like somebody killed him. Wished they'd done it when Noah was a little boy."

Mr. Man told the horse to "Giddup!" The wagon wheel came so close to Brer Fox that it rolled over the hairs growing out of his nose.

That didn't bother Brer Fox none. He did the same as before, and when Mr. Man come up on him this time, Mr. Man was perplexed. "How come there are all these dead foxes in the road this morning?"

Deciding that he better investigate, Mr. Man got down from the wagon. He felt Brer Fox's ears; they were right warm. He felt Brer Fox's neck; it was warm too. He examined Brer Fox's short ribs; they were all intact. He investigated Brer Fox's bones; they were solid. He turned Brer Fox over; Brer Fox was as limber as the double-jointed man who was in the carnival which came to town last year.

Mr. Man scratched his head. "What's going on here? This pig-eating chicken-stealer looks like he's dead, but ain't none of his bones broke. I didn't feel no bruises. On top of that, he's warm and limber. Something ain't right! This pig-stealing chicken-eater might be dead. Then again he might not be. I better make sure!"

Mr. Man took his whip, and *pow!* He hit Brer Fox so hard, it hurt me.

Brer Fox didn't need to hear the same message twice. While Mr. Man was drawing back his arm to hit him again, Brer Fox got on away from there. He ran so fast, his shadow had to take the bus home.

King Lion and Mr. Man

When the creatures heard what Mr. Man had done to Brer Fox, they decided to give Mr. Man all the room he wanted. That's what all of 'em decided excepting King Lion. He thought he was the baddest thing to walk the earth since body odor.

Now, I tell you the truth: Folks can come along with their whatchamacallits and they can do what's-his-name. They can walk big, talk big, and feel big. But one day something is going to come down the road that can walk bigger, talk bigger, and feel bigger, and when that day comes, trouble will snatch 'em slonchways and the bigger they are, the worser they get snatched. That's what happened to King Lion.

Everywhere he went, all he could hear was Mr. Man this and Mr. Man the other. King Lion got sick and tired of it. He shook his mane and roared so loud that it broke a couple of windowpanes up in heaven. "Where can I find this Mr. Man?" he wanted to know.

"You don't want to go messing with Mr. Man," Brer Dog told him.

"When I get through with Mr. Man he'll wish he was never born."

"King Lion, don't you start nothing with your mouth that your fists can't finish."

King Lion don't want to hear nothing like that, so he took off down the big road, looking for Mr. Man. The sun rose up and the sun shone hot, but King Lion, he kept on. The wind came up and filled the elements full of dust, but King Lion, he kept on. The rain drifted down and turned the dust into mud, but King Lion, he kept on. And then the sun burned hot once again.

After a while King Lion saw Mr. Steer grazing alongside the road.

"Howdy do, Mr. Steer."

"Howdy do, King Lion."

They exchanged some more pleasantries, inquired about
one another's children and kin, and then King Lion got
down to business.

"Look-a-here, Mr. Steer. You know anybody around these
parts named Mr. Man?"

"Sho' do. Knows him right well."

"Well, that's the one I'm looking for."

"What kind of business you got with Mr. Man?"

King Lion shook his mane and roared. "I'm going to
show him who's boss, that's what!"

"You best turn around and point your nose toward home,
King Lion. You asking for more trouble than you know
exists."

"Don't you know who I am?" King Lion roared. "I'm
the King! I'm the baddest thing in the whole world. I'm
so bad I know where the lights go when you turn 'em
out."

"What difference does that make?" Mr. Steer wanted to
know. "You see how big I am, don't you? I got long,
sharp horns too. But as big as I am and as sharp as my
horns are, Mr. Man caught me and hitched me to a wagon
and makes me haul wood and water and drives me anywhere he wants to. You best leave Mr. Man alone or he'll
hitch you up to a wagon."

King Lion shook his mane, roared, and went on off down
the road. In a little while he saw Mr. Horse eating grass
in the field. Him and Mr. Horse exchanged greetings and
inquired about one another's family tree, and then King
Lion got down to business.

"I know Mr. Man right well," said Mr. Horse when King Lion finished. "Been knowing him a long time. How come you want to make his acquaintance?"

"I'm going to show him who's boss in these parts."

Mr. Horse smiled. "You best leave Mr. Man alone. You see how big I am and how much strength I got and how tough my feet are. Well, Mr. Man come out here and put a saddle on my back and some rope in my mouth. Then he jumped on and now he rides me anywhere he wants to. He makes me run fast when he wants to go fast and walk slow when he wants to go slow. You mess with Mr. Man, he'll put a saddle on your back and a rope in your mouth too."

King Lion looked at Mr. Horse with disgust and went on down the road. He hadn't gone far when he saw Mr. Jack Sparrow sitting in a tree.

"What you doing in this neck of the woods, King Lion?"

King Lion ain't got time now for no pleasantries and family trees. "I'm looking for Mr. Man so I can show him who's the boss."

"He's cutting wood right around the next bend in the road. But if you take my advice, you'll let Mr. Man alone. You see how little I am and you know how high I can fly, but Mr. Man can fetch me out of the sky whenever he wants to. If you not careful, he'll fetch you too."

King Lion was so disgusted that he didn't even say a proper good-bye. He went on down the road and around the bend and there he saw a creature standing on his hindquarters, splitting wood.

King Lion had never seen Mr. Man and didn't know what one looked like. You probably seen Mr. Man, but I bet you ain't never seen one splitting wood and don't know what I'm talking about.

To split wood you need a maul and a wedge. A maul is like a sledgehammer, and a wedge is a heavy piece of iron that's got a sharp edge but is wide and thick in the back. You drive the wedge into the wood with the maul until the wood splits in half. You split the halves in halves and then you can use your ax to split it into kindling wood.

King Lion strutted over. "You know somebody called Mr. Man?"

Mr. Man put down his maul, narrowed his eyes, and looked at King Lion. "I know him as if he was my twin brother."

"I wants to meet him."

"Well," says Mr. Man, "stick your paw right in here and I'll go get him for you."

King Lion stuck his paw in the opening the wedge had

made. Soon as he done that, Mr. Man knocked the wedge out and the log snapped closed like it was the jaws of a shark. *Snap!*

"Ow! OW! OW!" hollered King Lion.

"Don't holler yet. Wait until I give you something good to scream about."

Mr. Man got his whip, same one he'd used on Brer Fox, and he laid into King Lion. He whipped King Lion until his arm was tired and then he let him go.

King Lion was hobbling around through the community on crutches for a long time after that but didn't none of the animals say a word to him about Mr. Man. He might not could whup Mr. Man, but he could still whup them.

Brer Fox and Brer Turtle

While all this was going on between King Lion and Mr. Man, Brer Fox was recuperating from the licking Mr. Man had given him. The weller Brer Fox got, the madder he got.

Don't make sense to me how come he got so mad. Mr. Man had caught him fair and square. Ain't a thing wrong with trying to play a trick on somebody, but if you get caught, take your licks like a man. Or should I say, like a woman? Tell you the truth, with all this here feminicity going around these days, I get scared that some of these feminicitists is going to put their mouth on these stories and next thing you know, we'll be hearing about the Fox-person and the Lionperson. But as long as I'm the one telling the tale, I say Brer Fox should've took his medicine like a man.

When Brer Fox was well enough to move about, he went looking to make somebody pay for what Mr. Man had done to him.

The first somebody he come upon was Brer Turtle. He should've walked past Brer Turtle. Brer Rabbit was the only creature with more smarts than Brer Turtle and sometimes Brer Rabbit had to scramble to keep up with the ol' Hardshell.

"Good morning, Brer Turtle. Where you been this long-come-short?"

"Just lounging around, Brer Fox. Just lounging around."

"You ain't looking too good, if the truth be known."

"I been lounging around and suffering." Brer Turtle sighed.

"What's the matter? Your eyes do look mighty red."

Brer Turtle shook his head. "Brer Fox, you don't know what trouble is."

Brer Fox could've written the book on being in trouble, but he didn't say nothing about that because he was intent on making trouble for Brer Turtle. "What's your problem?"

"I was out walking in the field the other day and Mr. Man come along and set the field on fire. You don't know what trouble is, Brer Fox, until you been caught in a fire."

"How'd you get out of the fire?"

"I had to sit and take it. Smoke sifted into my eyes and the fire scorched my back something terrible."

"And it looks to me, Brer Turtle, like that fire burned your tail off too."

"Naw, thank goodness. Here's my tail." Brer Turtle un-
curled his tail from underneath his shell and as soon as he
did, Brer Fox grabbed it.

"I gotcha, Brer Turtle. I gotcha!"

Brer Turtle begged Brer Fox to let him go, but Brer Fox
act like he deaf. Brer Turtle asked Brer Fox not to drown
him, but Brer Fox don't say nothing. Then Brer Turtle ask
Brer Fox to burn him because he's kinna used to fire. Brer
Fox don't say nothing. Finally Brer Fox carried him down
to the creek and dunked him under the water.

"Brer Fox! Brer Fox! Let go of that stump root you got hold of and catch me."

"I ain't got hold of no stump root! I got hold of your tail!"

"Grab me, Brer Fox! I'm drowning! I'm drowning! Turn loose that stump root and grab me!"

Brer Fox turned loose of Brer Turtle's tail, and Brer Turtle? Shucks, he just slid on down to the bottom of the creek—*kerblunkity-blink*—and went on home.

Brer Fox Gets Tricked by the Frogs

Sometimes I want to feel sorry for Brer Fox. There he was standing on the bank of the creek and wasn't nothing he could do except watch Brer Turtle slowly sink to the bottom.

When Brer Turtle got to his home, he said, *"I-doom-a-ker-kum-mer-ker."* That's Turtle talk. I could tell you what it means 'cause I know creature talk. You been around much as I have, you'll know the language of all the creatures. I even know Cockroach talk but I ain't never thought of nothing to say to a cockroach so I don't talk it none.

Brer Turtle knowed English wasn't good enough to say all that was on his mind and that's how come he switched to Turtle talk. *"I-doom-a-ker-kum-mer-ker."* It's best I don't translate that.

Brer Bullfrog was sitting off in the weeds and when he heard Brer Turtle, he hollered back: *"Jug-a-rum-kum-dum! Jug-a-rum-kum-dum!"*

Another Frog yelled, *"Knee-deep! Knee-deep!"*

Brer Bullfrog said, *"Don't you believe him! Don't you believe him!"*

Then, from way down at the bottom of the creek, Brer Turtle said, *"I-doom-a-ker-kum-mer-ker!"*

The Frog yelled: *"Wade in! Wade in!"*

Brer Bullfrog croaked: *"There you'll find your brother! There you'll find your brother!"*

Brer Fox was listening to all this carrying on and he looked into the water, and sho' 'nuf! There was a Fox looking up at him. Brer Fox leaned over to shake hands with the Fox in the water, and the next thing he knew, he went head over tail and right smack in the water. *Kersplash!*

Brer Bullfrog hollered: *"You found your brother! You found your brother!"*

And from way down at the bottom of the creek Brer Turtle said: *"I-doom-a-ker-kum-mer-ker! I-doom-a-ker-kum-mer-ker!"*

Brer Bear Gets Tricked by Brer Frog

A few days later Brer Fox was telling some of the other creatures about his recent misfortunes. All the other creatures sympathized with him, all of 'em, that is, except Brer Bear.

"You got to be mighty dumb to get fooled by Brer Frog," he said. "If Brer Frog got any brains at all, they in his bass voice."

Brer Fox say, "Let's find out how supple your brains are. Why don't you go on down there to the creek and see if you can get some frog for supper?"

Brer Bear say he didn't think frog was kosher, but then again, he wasn't Jewish so he reckon it don't matter. He went and got his ax and headed for the creek.

Time he got there he saw Brer Bullfrog sitting on the creek bank. Without so much as a "Good morning" or a "How's the family" Brer Bear grabbed him. Then he remembered his manners.

"Good morning, Brer Bullfrog. How's your family? I hope they well and you done took out plenty insurance, 'cause in five minutes you'll be history. Your days of tricking folks have come to an end."

"What did I do?" Brer Bullfrog wanted to know.

"Ain't you the one what tricked Brer Fox into falling into the creek?"

Brer Bullfrog said, "It takes two to make a trick. The tricker and the trickee. Ain't my fault if Brer Fox make such a good trickee."

"I ain't got time for a whole lot of philosophy or psychology. What I'm studying today is frogology." Brer Bear started snapping his jaws and foaming at the mouth.

"Brer Bear! Brer Bear! Please let me off this time. I promise I won't play no more tricks, no matter how good a trickee come along. And not only that. If you let me go, I'll show you a tree that's just oozing with honey."

Brer Bear started gnashing his teeth.

"Please, Brer Bear! Please let me go!"

Brer Bear was too hungry to be thinking about any letting go.

"All right, Brer Bear. I know my time done come. I see

you brought your ax with you too. Just do me this favor. Carry me up to that big flat rock which overlooks the creek. I want to look down and see my family one last time. After I see 'em, you can take your ax and send me to that big lotus pad in the sky."

Well, Brer Bear wasn't a hardhearted man, so he carried Brer Bullfrog to the rock and put him down. Brer Bullfrog creeped to the edge and peered over like he was looking for his kinfolk.

Brer Bear took a deep breath, picked up his ax, and swung it round and round over his head—once, twice, three times—and come down with the ax as hard as he could.

Brer Bear hit that rock so hard it rattled the TV antenna on the Lord's house up in heaven. When he lifted the ax up and looked for a smashed Brer Bullfrog, wasn't a thing

there except a hole. Brer Frog had leaped off the rock, done a back somersault half-double gainer with a twist of lemon, and gone right into the water without so much as a splash.

And just about the time Brer Bear realized that Brer Bullfrog had found another trickee, Brer Bear heard Brer Bullfrog sing out:

Ingle-go-jang, my joy, my joy—
Ingle-go-jang, my joy!
I'm right at home, my joy, my joy—
Ingle-go-jang, my joy, my joy!

To your ears that song might sound funny, 'cause folks don't be using words like that. But to us what knows creature talk, that was a mighty serious song. If folks knew as much about creature talk and Bullfrog language as they used to, they probably wouldn't let me put that song in this story.

Brer Bear, Brer Turtle, and the Rope-Pulling Contest

Brer Bear should've had more sense than to mess with the water creatures. Water creatures got more sense than people, 'cause they done figured out how to live in the water. If it's left to me, we never will figure that out. I stay as far away from water as I can. I don't even speak to my bathtub.

The other reason Brer Bear should've left the water creatures alone was because whenever anybody messed with them, it made Brer Turtle angry, and the last thing anybody wants to do is get Brer Turtle upset.

A week or so later, all the animals were sitting around in Miz Meadows's yard. Well, you know how it is when men get around the ladies. Whenever there's a lady around, men can't think about nothing else but showing off.

Brer Rabbit started flapping his gums about how he was the swiftest of all the animals. Brer Fox said he was the sharpest. Brer Wolf said he was the most vigorous. Brer Bear said he was the strongest.

That was a little too much for Brer Turtle. "Brer Rabbit, everybody know I beat you in the big race, so don't be talking about how fast you are. Brer Fox, I know a thing or two about you but I don't want to embarrass you. Brer Wolf, if the Lord told us to turn in our brains for money, you'd be in debt. And Brer Bear, the only thing strong about you is your breath."

What did Brer Turtle want to say that for? Brer Bear rose up, and he looked big as a mountain and four times stronger. He walked around the circle flexing his muscles and little beads of sweat started popping out on the brows of the creatures, except for Brer Turtle. He was giggling.

"When you through acting like you practicing to be in the Mr. Universe contest, let's find out who's the strongest."

"How we gon' do that?" Brer Bear wanted to know.

"We'll have a rope-pulling contest."

All the creatures agreed that sounded like a good idea. The only problem was, they didn't have a rope. Miz Meadows say she got plenty rope.

"Then, let the good times roll," said Brer Turtle.

There wasn't enough space to have a decent rope-pulling contest in Miz Meadows's yard, so they went down to the creek.

When they got there, Brer Turtle took one end of the rope and gave the other to Brer Bear. "Looks to me like when we get this rope stretched out, Brer Bear, you'll be up there in the woods. When I see the slack go out of the rope, I'll give a holler and you start pulling, and we'll see who's the strongest."

Brer Bear and the other creatures went up in the woods. Then Brer Turtle took his end of the rope and dove into the water. He swam down to the bottom and tied the rope around a great big limb which was stuck in the mud. Then he swam back up to the creek bank.

"I'm ready, Brer Bear! You can start pulling!" he hollered.

Brer Bear wrapped the rope around his hand, gave Miz Meadows a big wink, and started pulling. Nothing happened.

"I said you could start pulling, Brer Bear!"

Brer Bear took both hands and pulled harder. The rope didn't budge.

"Are you pulling yet, Brer Bear?" yelled Brer Turtle.

Brer Bear turned around, put the rope over his shoulder, and pulled. Nothing happened. The rest of the creatures decided to give Brer Bear a hand, and they grabbed hold of the rope and pulled. Nothing happened. Finally Brer Bear decided there wasn't nothing he could do and let the rope go.

As soon as Brer Turtle saw the rope go slack, he dove down in the water, untied the rope from the limb, and swam back up with it. When Brer Bear and the rest of the creatures got down to the creek bank, Brer Turtle was laying there huffing and puffing like he was about to die.

"That last pull you give on the rope was mighty powerful, Brer Bear. Little bit more and I think you would've had me."

Brer Turtle Takes Care of Brer Buzzard

Nothing in the world gets your appetite going like tricking folks, and after tricking Brer Bear, Brer Turtle was hungry.

I don't know about these here modern turtles, but back in my day, the Turtle loved to eat honey. But being so little, even if he found a bee tree, he couldn't get the honey, 'cause he couldn't climb the tree.

Well, after he had shown Brer Bear who was the strongest, he went on off down the road. His mind was wrapping itself around pictures of golden honey when he happened to run into Brer Buzzard.

They shook hands and asked about one another's family and like that. Then it occurred to Brer Turtle that Brer Buzzard might be the man he was looking for.

He explained to Brer Buzzard how he couldn't keep his mind off getting some honey. Brer Buzzard said that *his* mind was just about to land on the very thing Brer Turtle's mind couldn't get off of.

"Then you and me is of one mind, Brer Buzzard. Let's join forces. Two heads are better than one, especially when they on different bodies. You fly around and look for a bee tree and I'll creep and crawl like I always do and hunt down here on the ground."

Brer Buzzard said that sounded like a good idea, and off they went.

Before long Brer Turtle came to a field and found a great big beehive on the ground. He wiggled his head inside and almost drowned in all the honey. He wiggled out and looked to see if Brer Buzzard was around. Brer Buzzard wasn't even a speck in the sky.

Brer Turtle thought for a minute. "Brer Buzzard is used to eating that sweet honey which you can only find in the tops of the trees. This honey what's been on the ground is at least Grade B and might even be Grade Z. What kind of friend would I be to offer honey to Brer Buzzard that ain't as sweet and good as what he's used to? I might as well eat this honey instead of insulting Brer Buzzard with it."

Brer Turtle crawled inside the beehive and proceeded to have himself a honey feast. When he was all done, he wriggled out and licked the honey off his feet so Brer Buzzard wouldn't know he'd found any.

Then it occurred to him that there was probably honey on his back. He stretched out his neck and tried to lick it off, but his neck wouldn't stretch that far. He leaned up against a tree and tried to scrape it off, but nothing doing. He rolled around on his back and tried to get it off, but no luck.

Just as Brer Turtle was deciding that he'd better get away from there before Brer Buzzard come back, he saw him coming in for a landing, his black wings spread out like thunderclouds!

Brer Turtle ran to the beehive, built a fire inside, and ran out shouting "Brer Buzzard! Brer Buzzard! Come here and see how much honey I found. There's so much honey in there, it dripped all over my back like a waterfall. Come quick, Brer Buzzard. You go in and get your half and then I'll get mine."

Brer Buzzard chuckled. "You found that honey just in time, 'cause I got mighty hungry flying around up there."

Brer Buzzard squeezed himself in the beehive. Soon as he was inside, Brer Turtle stopped up the opening with a big rock.

In a few minutes the fire Brer Turtle had built inside got going good. Brer Buzzard hollered out, "Ow! Something is biting me, Brer Turtle!"

"It's the bees biting you, Brer Buzzard. Flop your wings and drive 'em off."

Brer Buzzard started flopping his wings, which didn't do nothing but fan the fire and make it burn bigger and hotter. Before long there wasn't nothing left of Brer Buzzard but the ends of his big wing feathers.

When the ashes cooled down, Brer Turtle took the feathers and made 'em into quill pipes. He played a tune on the quill pipes and sang this song:

> *I fooled you, I fooled you, I fooled you,*
> *Po' Buzzard;*
> *Po' Buzzard I fooled you, I fooled you,*
> *I fooled you.*

If you was to say that wasn't much of a song, I would have to go along with you. But it sho' was the truth.

Brer Fox Wants to Make Music

You probably wondering how Brer Turtle could make music on Buzzard quills. Well, I tell you the truth: I don't know. But 'cause I don't know don't mean that Brer Turtle didn't know, and obviously he did know, 'cause the story say that what he was doing.

Brer Fox didn't know either, but when he heard Brer Turtle playing such pretty music on them quills, he wanted the quills for himself.

He begged and begged Brer Turtle to sell him the quills, but Brer Turtle say, nothing doing. Brer Fox asked Brer Turtle if he could borrow 'em for a week so he could learn how to play pretty music. Brer Turtle just keep on playing.

He asked Brer Turtle to let him look at the quills up close. He had some goose feathers at home and might could make him a set of his own. Brer Turtle thought that was a good idea, 'cause then Brer Fox would stop pestering him.

Brer Turtle held out the quills so Brer Fox could see 'em close up. The minute he did, Brer Fox snatched them quills and ran away.

Brer Turtle hollered, "Thief! Thief!" Everybody wondered how come Brer Turtle was wasting his breath saying the obvious.

Brer Turtle was miserable without his quills. He sat down in the road looking like he needed a dime to call his therapist.

The next morning when Brer Fox come dancing down the road playing on the quills, Brer Turtle was right where Brer Fox had left him. Brer Fox danced around Brer Turtle just a-playing and a-singing:

He fooled po' Brer Buzzard, he did,
But I fooled him. Yes, I fooled him.

The next day Brer Turtle was sitting on a log when Brer Fox came along playing that same song on the quills. Brer Turtle pretend like he ain't heard nothing.

Brer Fox came closer and played louder. Brer Turtle's eyes were closed but his ears was wide open. He listened and listened and when Brer Fox got close, Brer Turtle snapped at Brer Fox's foot.

But he missed. Brer Fox laughed and danced away.

The next morning Brer Turtle went down in a mudhole and smeared himself all over with mud. When he finished he looked like a clod of dirt. Then he crawled under a log where he knew Brer Fox came every morning.

Brer Turtle hadn't been there long before Brer Fox came. He sat down on the log and Brer Turtle stuck his neck out and grabbed Brer Fox's big toe!

They tell me that when a Turtle grabs on to something, it has got to thunder before he'll let go. Brer Fox didn't know nothing about that, 'cause he was in so much pain.

"Let me go, Brer Turtle. Please let me go!"

Brer Turtle talked way down in his throat. "Give me my quills."

"Let me go and I'll get 'em."

"Give me my quills."

"How can I give you the quills with you hanging on my toe?"

"Give me my quills."

Brer Fox wondered if Brer Turtle had gone crazy, 'cause that seemed to be all he could say. Brer Fox hollered for his oldest boy.

"Toby! Toby!"

"What you want, Daddy?"

"Bring Brer Turtle's quills!"

"What'd you say? Bring the fur and the cleaning bills?"

"No, you dummy! Bring Brer Turtle's quills!"

"What you say? Water done spill?"

"No, fool! Bring Brer Turtle's quills."

"What you say, Daddy? Go hurdle the hills?"

Well, it went on this way until Miz Fox began to wonder what all the racket was about. She listened and knew that Brer Fox was hollering for the quills. She took them down there and gave them to Brer Turtle.

Brer Turtle let go of Brer Fox's toe, but for a long time after that everybody could see Brer Turtle's autograph on Brer Fox's foot.

The Pimmerly Plum

Brer Turtle had his quills back, but he was angry. He decided to teach Brer Fox a lesson so that he would stay taught.

You know what Brer Turtle did? Well, he didn't scare him. It was worse than that. He didn't hurt him. It was worse than that. He didn't kill him. It was worse than that. You know what he did? He made a fool out of him.

A few days later Brer Turtle was going down the road. It was one of them hot days and he was huffing and puffing and blowing and sweating, and mostly he was cussing, but I can't put that in the story.

He made his way to the creek, crawled in, and cooled off. After a while he crawled out and settled in the shade of a big tree. Brer Turtle carries his house with him, and when he wants to go to sleep, he just shuts the door and pulls down the shades and he's as snug as a black cat under the couch.

He slept and he slept. He didn't know how long he slept, and since I wasn't there that day, I don't either. But he woke up suddenly, 'cause somebody had picked him up and was shaking him like they were trying to turn him to soup right there in his shell. Brer Turtle kept the door shut tight and listened.

When the shaking stopped, Brer Turtle cracked the door open to see who it was. Wasn't nobody but Brer Fox holding him up in the air.

Brer Turtle opened the door wide and stuck his head out and he was laughing as hard as he could. "Well, well, well. Look who done caught me. Ain't none other than

Brer Fox. You picked a good time to come along, Brer Fox, 'cause I'm so full and feeling so good, I can't do a thing to you."

"How come you so full and feeling so good?" Brer Fox wanted to know.

"I just finished eating Pimmerly Plums."

The Pimmerly Plum was the hardest-to-find fruit there was. Besides Brer Rabbit and Brer Turtle, none of the other creatures had ever even seen it, but they'd sho' 'nuf heard about it. It was supposed to be sweeter than a kiss, more juicy than ripe grapes, and tastier than a plate of waffles dripping with maple syrup.

Just the sound of the words *Pimmerly Plum* sent Brer Fox to daydreaming, and without even knowing he was doing it, he set Brer Turtle down on the ground. Brer Fox's eyes started rolling around in his head and he was dribbling at the mouth.

"Where's the Pimmerly Plum?" he wanted to know.

Brer Turtle laughed a big laugh.

"What you laughing about?"

"Why, Brer Fox! You standing right under the tree."

I got to explain something here. I know practically none of y'all ever seen a sycamore tree. Ain't no sycamore trees in the city and if there was, probably one of them muggers would steal 'em. If you was to ever see a sycamore tree, you'd recognize it immediately, because little round balls hang by a twig from the ends of their branches.

Brer Turtle pointed to the balls and said, "Them's the Pimmerly Plums, Brer Fox."

The balls were too high for Brer Fox to get. What was he going to do?

"That's where being as full of energy as you are don't

work to your advantage, Brer Fox. If you was a Slickum Slow-Come like me, wouldn't be no problem."

"Brer Turtle, what're you talking about?"

"Wouldn't do no good for me to tell you. Nimble heel, restless mind. You ain't got the time to wait and get 'em, Brer Fox."

"Brer Turtle, I got all the time in the world for the Pimmerly Plum."

Brer Turtle shook his head. "Naw, I know you. If I tell you how to get them, you'll start beating your gums and telling all the other creatures. Next thing I know, the Pimmerly Plum will have gone the way of Brer Dodo Bird."

"I wouldn't do that, Brer Turtle. I won't say a word to a living soul. A dead one either."

Brer Turtle closed his eyes like he was thinking. Finally he said, "All right, Brer Fox. I believe you. Whenever I want some of the Pimmerly Plum, this is what I do. I come here to the tree and I get right under it. I put my head back and shut my eyes. Then I open my mouth as wide as I can, and when the Pimmerly Plum is ready to drop, it drops right in my mouth. All you got to do is be patient and don't move."

Brer Fox didn't wait to hear another word. He sat down on his haunches beneath the tree, reared back his head, closed his eyes, and opened his mouth.

Brer Turtle started to laugh but then decided he could laugh louder and longer if he was to do it at home, which is where he went.

You know, it's a curious thing about this story. Ain't nobody ever told me how long Brer Fox sat there with his head reared back, eyes closed and mouth open. For all I know, he might still be there.

Brer Turtle Takes Flying Lessons

Brer Turtle decided to reward himself for having gotten rid of Brer Fox for a while, so he went looking for Brer Buzzard, 'cause he wanted to take flying lessons.

I know. You thought Brer Buzzard got burned up. So what if he did? What makes you think *that* Brer Buzzard was this Brer Buzzard or that this Brer Buzzard was that Brer Buzzard? Sometimes that is that and this is this. Other times this is that and that is the other and everything else is chocolate pudding.

Now, where was I? Oh, yes. Brer Turtle started pestering Brer Buzzard about giving him flying lessons. Brer Buzzard said Brer Turtle couldn't learn to fly because there was too much of him in the same place. But Brer Turtle wasn't about to take no for an answer. Finally Brer Buzzard said he'd do it.

Brer Turtle was ready right then, but Brer Buzzard said he had to go get his pilot's license renewed and it was also his day to get his hair shampooed and nails manicured and he'd see Brer Turtle the next day.

Next morning, just as King Sun was peeking his left eye over the topside of the world, Brer Buzzard sailed in. He squatted down on the grass next to Brer Turtle. Brer Turtle huffed and puffed and finally made it onto Brer Buzzard's back.

Brer Buzzard started off real easy. He caught a nice gentle current of wind under his big wings and soared around for a while over the fields and the river. Brer Turtle said that flying was might nice. A few more lessons and he'd be ready to do it on his own.

Every morning for the next few days Brer Turtle took a ride on Brer Buzzard's back. "Tomorrow morning, Brer

Buzzard, when we get up in the air, I'm gon' do my own flying."

"Whatever you say, Brer Turtle."

Next morning came and Brer Buzzard took Brer Turtle on up. Brer Buzzard got so high in the sky that you could hear the stars yawning as they was going to bed. 'Long about the time King Sun was finishing his first cup of coffee, Brer Buzzard swooped and slid out from under Brer Turtle.

Brer Turtle flapped his feet and wagged his head and shook his tail, but that didn't help him one bit. He turned upside down and right-side up and sideways over sideways

and hit the ground—*ka-blam-a-blam-blam-blam!* If his shell hadn't been so strong, Brer Turtle would've busted wide open.

He lay there huffing and puffing and groaning like the next minute was going to be his last.

Brer Buzzard sailed down and landed next to Brer Turtle. "How you feel?"

"I'm ruined, Brer Buzzard. My back ain't never gon' be the same."

"I tried to tell you that you didn't have the requirements for flying."

"Brer Buzzard, just hush up! I flew as good as you or any of the other winged creatures. But you forgot to teach me how to land! Flying is easy, but landing can be mighty hard on a body."

Brer Buzzard and Brer Hawk

Brer Buzzard is one of the ugliest creatures in nature. If ugly was money, Brer Buzzard would've been the richest thing to ever walk the earth. But if being ugly wasn't bad enough, Brer Buzzard never did score above the single digits on an IQ test. I threw out an empty can of peas the other day what had more sense than Brer Buzzard.

Brer Buzzard could fly high and he could fly low and he could fly around in great big circles. But he didn't have sense enough to stay dry when it rained. On rainy days Brer Buzzard would find a big tall pine tree to sit in. It would rain and the wind would blow and Brer Buzzard would look as raggedy as a mop which has seen a few too many kitchen floors. Brer Buzzard would say, "When the wind stops blowing and the rain stops dripping, I going to build me a house. No doubt about it. And I'm gon' make that house tight to keep the rain and wind out."

The next day when the sky would be all dried out and the wind was curled up again in that big pot the Lord keeps it in and King Sun would turn his light on again, Brer Buzzard would spread his wings, stretch his neck, and dry himself off. "Ain't no point in building a house to-day," he'd say, " 'cause it ain't raining no more." The only thing Brer Buzzard wasn't dumb about was eating.

One time Brer Hawk was sailing around on his pretty wings looking for something to eat, and he saw Brer Buzzard sitting on a dead limb, looking lazy and lonesome.

Brer Hawk flew down. "What's happening, Brer Buzzard?"

Brer Buzzard shook his head. "Ain't doing too good, Brer Hawk. I'm po' and hungry."

"Well, if you hungry, why don't you go find some food? You ain't got to hunt your food like I do. Ol' Boy do your hunting for you, and Ol' Boy ain't never took a day off from work."

Brer Buzzard shook his head. "That's true, Brer Hawk, but I'm gon' wait on the Lord."

Brer Hawk laughed. "You best go get some breakfast and then come back and wait. It's a lot easier to wait on the Lord when you got something in your stomach."

Brer Buzzard shook his head. "I want to be here so the Lord can provide."

Brer Hawk chuckled. "Whatever you say. You got your ways and I got mine. I see some chickens down there in

Mr. Man's yard. I'm gon' swoop down and get one and then I'll come back and wait with you."

Brer Hawk spread his great wings and took off. Brer Buzzard scrunched his neck down between his shoulders and looked more lonesome than ever. But he kept one eye on Brer Hawk.

Brer Hawk flew way up in the sky. He flew so high that King Sun started to put a For Sale sign in his front yard, 'cause he didn't want to have nothing to do with Brer Hawk's sharp talons and beak. Brer Hawk wasn't thinking about King Sun. He had his sharp eyes on them chickens.

When he had decided on the one that looked the plumpest and juiciest, he tucked in his wings and shot down from the sky like he'd been fired from a gun. He was going so fast that the air turned cold as he flew down through the sky and all the clouds had to put on their winter coats. But Brer Hawk was going too fast for his own good because his aim was a little off and he was too close to the ground to do anything about it.

Po' Brer Hawk. Instead of landing on that chicken he landed on the point of the fence post and that fence post went through him like it was a sword.

Brer Buzzard looked down at Brer Hawk. Brer Hawk don't move. Brer Buzzard wait and watch some more. Brer Hawk still don't move. He was stone dead.

"I knew the Lord would provide," Brer Buzzard said, and he flew on down to where Brer Hawk was waiting for him.

———————————

Brer Buzzard Bites the Dust—Again

The second time Brer Buzzard come to an unfortunate end was almost like the first time. But anybody what ain't got enough sense to know how to stay dry when it's raining don't deserve no better.

The way it come about was like this:

One time Brer Wolf and Brer Fox got to arguing about something. Wasn't nothing important, 'cause Brer Wolf and Brer Fox didn't know nothing important. But what ain't important to you and me is earth shaking to somebody else, and that's the way it was with Brer Wolf and Brer Fox.

Brer Wolf said it was so and Brer Fox said it wasn't so. Brer Wolf said was, and Brer Fox said wasn't, and they got to wasing and wasn'ting something fierce until Brer Wolf called Brer Fox dumb and Brer Fox said to Brer Wolf, "Your mama is dumb." Look out! You don't be talking about nobody's mama, not even Brer Wolf's.

Brer Wolf don't say nothing else, leastways not with his mouth. But he had a left jab, a right cross, left uppercut, and right hook that used up a whole lot of words in the dictionary. Brer Fox was scared that Brer Wolf might start using some of them words what's in the encyclopedia, and he took off.

Brer Wolf was right with him, snapping at his tail. Brer Fox knew he had to find someplace to hide. He spied a hollow tree and dove in head first. Brer Wolf snapped at him, but he was just in time to be too late.

Brer Wolf sat down next to the tree and began to think on how to get Brer Fox out. When he couldn't think of nothing, he decided that it would be just as good to keep Brer Fox in.

He gathered up a whole bunch of rocks and filled the hole in the tree until Brer Fox was sealed in as tight as if he was in a grave.

Brer Buzzard was flopping around up in the elements and he saw Brer Wolf sealing up the hole in the tree.

"I believe I better go down and investigate," Brer Buzzard said to himself. "If Brer Wolf is hiding his dinner and planning on coming back for it later, he has put his dinner in the wrong place. But I ain't gon' tell him that."

Brer Buzzard flopped on down. "What you doing, Brer Wolf?"

"Making a tombstone."

Any mention of death brings a smile to Brer Buzzard's face. "Who's dead?" he asked, barely able to contain his joy.

"Brer Fox."

"When did he die?"

"He ain't dead yet, but he won't last long in there. He's all yours, Brer Buzzard." Brer Wolf brushed his hands and clothes off and went on home like a man who'd just finished a good day's work.

Brer Buzzard put his ear close to the tree. He could hear Brer Fox inside crying something awful. Brer Buzzard might not have had sense enough to know how to stay dry, but he knew dead folks don't cry. So he flew on off.

Bright and early the next morning Brer Buzzard came back. He put his ear to the tree. He didn't hear a thing. He waited a while, then listened again. Still don't hear nothing. Then he sang a song:

> *Boo, boo, book, my filler-ma-loo,*
> *Man out here with news for you.*

He put his ear to the tree and listened. Brer Fox sang back:

> *Go away, go away, my little jug of beer,*
> *The news you bring, I heard last year.*

I ain't exactly sure what kind of beer it was, but I know it wasn't Miller Lite or Bud. Seems like I remember somebody telling me it was root beer, but whether it was caffeine free or low cal, I don't know.

When Brer Buzzard heard Brer Fox sing back, he figured that he wasn't dead, which was good figuring. So Brer Buzzard went on about his business.

Bright and early the next morning Brer Buzzard came back. He sang his song and Brer Fox sang his song. Brer Buzzard don't mind. He's a very patient man. Waiting on Ol' Boy had never tired him out.

Brer Fox was not a patient man, especially when he was hungry and his navel and his backbone were carrying on deep philosophical conversations. Brer Fox knew he had to come up with a plan to get out of there.

Bright and early the next morning here come Brer Buzzard. He went up to the tree and stuck his ear against it. Don't hear nothing. then he sang out:

> *Boo, boo, boo, my filler-ma-loo,*
> *Man out here with news for you!*

He listened at the tree. Don't hear nothing. He listen awhile longer. Still don't hear nothing. A big grin spread over his face.

He started taking the rocks out of the hole. He'd take a few rocks out and listen. Don't hear nothing. He'd take a few more out and listen again. It went on this way until the hole was uncovered.

The minute it was, Brer Fox came charging out like it was Judgment Day and he was gon' be late getting through the Pearly Gates. He grabbed Brer Buzzard by the neck and what he did after that is too horrible to talk about. But I can tell you that by the time Brer Fox got through, there wasn't enough of Brer Buzzard left for a funeral.

The Wise Bird and the Foolish Bird

Once there was a Wise Bird and a Foolish Bird. Both lived in the same country and both used the same forest.

One day the Wise Bird lighted in the tree where the Foolish Bird was sitting.

The Wise Bird looked at the Foolish Bird admiringly. "You are one good-looking bird," he said. "You are long in the leg and deep in the craw. You stand so tall and erect. You look like you're going to live a long time."

The Foolish Bird swelled with pride. "Well, I don't like to brag, but it's always nice when others recognize your good qualities."

"I've always been one to give credit where credit is due," the Wise Bird said. "However, I think there's one area where I can outdo you."

"And what might that be?"

"I can go longer than you can without drinking water."

The Foolish Bird was indignant. "I doubt that very seriously."

"How about we have a little contest, then?" proposed

the Wise Bird. "Let's see who can go the longest without drinking water."

The Foolish Bird stuck out his neck and tossed his head and laughed. "I'll beat you all day every day."

The Wise Bird handed the Foolish Bird a horn. "Here. You take this horn and go up in that tree on the creek side. I'll take this horn and go up in a tree on the hillside. We'll see how long we can go without drinking. When I blow on my horn, you blow on yours and answer me. Me blow, you blow, and then we'll both blow."

The Foolish Bird strutted around on the limb. "I'll beat you all day every day."

The next morning the Wise Bird and the Foolish Bird took their horns and went to their trees.

The Foolish Bird was in the tree by the creek, and before long he discovered that there wasn't a thing to eat in that tree.

The Wise Bird's tree was covered with bark, and the bark was crawling with bugs, ants, and worms. The Wise Bird ate and ate and ate until he thought he was going to burst.

The Foolish Bird was beginning to feel tired from hunger. He sat down and felt more tired. He got up and was still tired. He stood on one leg and then on the other. He tucked his head beneath his wing, but no matter what he did, he was still tired.

The Wise Bird felt so good that he took a little nap, and when he woke up he felt even better. He picked up his horn and tooted it loud and clear:

Tay-tay, tenando wansando waneanzo!

The Foolish Bird was tired but he took his horn and blew:

Tay-tay, tenando wansando waneanzo!

Along about sundown the Wise Bird was hungry again. He ate more bugs and ants and worms, which were crawling all over his tree, and when he was full he felt very, very good. Then he picked up his horn and tooted it loud and clear:

Tay-tay, tenando wansando waneanzo!

The Foolish Bird picked up his horn and answered back, but the sound of his horn was weak.

The next morning when King Sun came up, the Wise Bird ate some more bugs, ants, and worms. Then he drank the dew off the leaves, belched a couple of times, and chuckled. He picked up his horn and started blowing. He blew so good that some of the other birds wondered if Louis Armstrong had come to town.

The Foolish Bird tooted back, but his toot was so faint you could hardly hear it.

When dinnertime came the Wise Bird ate his fill. Then he picked up his horn and did a pretty good imitation of Miles Davis playing "Round about Midnight." The Foolish Bird tooted back but it wasn't as loud as a whisper.

When Sister Moon came up that night, the Wise Bird played a couple of choruses of "Fly Me to the Moon." This time he didn't hear a toot from the Foolish Bird.

The Wise Bird flew over to the tree by the creek, and there was the Foolish Bird as dead as dead can get.

The Wise Bird played "When the Saints Go Marching In" and went on about his business.

The Most-Beautiful-Bird in-the-World Contest

This story is about the most beautiful bird in the whole world. She's gone away now and can't nobody find her.

Some called her the Coogly Bird. Others called her the Cow-Cow Bird. Still others said she was the Coo-Coo Bird. Call her what you please. Call her when you please. It ain't gon' make no difference. If calling would've fetched her back, she would be here now. But the birds been calling for her from that day to this and she ain't come yet. She was the prettiest bird there ever was and ever will be.

Way back yonder when the clouds were thicker than they are now, back when the sun didn't have to go to bed at night to keep from being tired the next day, the creatures didn't have much to do, especially the birds. They flew around and played games; they ate their meals together without getting into squabbles, and spent all their time socializing with one another.

After a while having peace began to get on their nerves and they started getting into squabbles with one another.

One day Miz Red Bird announced that she was the prettiest thing to sit on a limb since apple blossoms. What she want to say that for? Miz Blue Bird said Miz Red Bird better get her mirror checked, 'cause it had started lying to her. Miz Jay Bird said, uh-uh, wasn't nobody more glamorouser than her. Brer Hawk come sticking his lip in the matter and cast a vote for himself. And you might not believe this, but Brer Buzzard say that the other birds didn't know what pretty was until they got a good look at him. The arguing got so bad that war was about to break out.

Miz Wren, Miz Blue Bird, and Miz Robin got together to figure out how to stop all the arguing and fighting. They thought and they thought and they studied and they studied, but they couldn't come up with a solution.

After a while Miz Wren said, "I got an idea. Why don't we go home and ask our menfolk what they think. You know how men are. They know everything except what they know, and that's what they done forgot."

Miz Robin and Miz Blue Bird said that was the smartest thing they'd ever heard.

The next morning Miz Wren, Miz Robin, and Miz Blue Bird got together again. Miz Robin said she'd asked her husband and he said she best help him hunt bugs for the children and stop wasting time on what don't matter. Miz Blue Bird said that when she asked her husband, he said he needed some clean underwear to put on for work the next day. Miz Wren said that when she asked her husband, he wanted to know how come she didn't cook nothing every day but worm casserole with Parmesan cheese. She said she told him that anytime he wanted to try eating in somebody else's kitchen, he was more than welcome. Then he said, "You should have a big gathering of all the lady birds, have everybody parade around and let somebody pick out the prettiest one, and that would be that. If the judge say the Owl was the prettiest, then wasn't no dis-puting about it. If the judge say the Buzzard was the pret-tiest, well, that was how it was going to be. Once the

matter is settled, I'll buy you this new cookbook I saw—
Three Hundred and Sixty-five Ways to Cook Worms."

Miz Wren, Miz Robin, and Miz Blue Jay didn't know
about the cookbook, but they thought having a contest
was a good idea. They talked it over with the other birds,
and everybody agreed.

Then they discussed who the judge should be. They
quickly agreed there wasn't nobody better for the job than
Brer Rabbit, 'cause he wasn't a bird eater and his decision
wouldn't be influenced by his stomach.

The day for the contest came. Brer Rabbit was sitting
in a big chair and all the birds started coming in. They
had on their Guccis and Puccis and K mart best and were
wearing high heels and pearls and dangly earrings and smiles
left over from the Miss America contest.

The parade had barely started, though, when Brer Rabbit shook his head.

All the birds stopped. "What's the matter, Brer Rabbit?
How come you shaking your head like something is the
matter?"

Brer Rabbit shook his head again. "Can't be no contest
because one bird is missing." He got up out of his chair
and made a courteous bow. He looked so good that Miz
Swamp Owl's mouth started to water. Rabbit meat was
the tastiest thing in the world to her, but she controlled
herself.

"Wait a minute, Brer Rabbit!" the birds called out.
"Who's missing?"

"Where's Miz Coo-Coo Bird?" he asked.

Didn't nobody know.

Brer Rabbit said, "You gon' have to postpone the contest until somebody can get word to Miz Coo-Coo Bird.

She's got to be in the contest. If she ain't, she might not go along with my decision. If you want all the squabbling to stop, she got to be here. Ain't no two ways about that."

Some of the birds say the contest can go on without Miz Coo-Coo Bird 'cause she wasn't nothing to look at anyway. But they finally agreed there couldn't be no contest if all the birds wasn't there.

Well, time went on just like it does now, except that back in them days mealtime came a whole lot sooner. Some of the birds went looking for Miz Coo-Coo Bird. The rest spent as much time as they could at Brer Rabbit's house trying to get him to see them through their eyes.

It took 'em about a week, but they found Miz Coo-Coo Bird at home, which is where they should've gone first. When the birds saw her, they were surprised. Miz Coo-Coo Bird didn't have on a stitch of clothes. Where there should've been feathers there wasn't nothing but fuzz.

"How come you didn't come to the contest?" the birds asked.

"Look at me! I ain't got nothing to wear."

"Well, we sorry about that, but we got to have all the birds at the contest so it'll be fair."

Miz Coo-Coo Bird shook her head and went on back to cleaning out the oven. The birds persuaded and pleaded and argued. Finally Miz Coo-Coo Bird said, "If y'all will lend me something to wear, I'll come."

The birds went around to all the other birds and asked each one to loan Miz Coo-Coo Bird a feather. Miss Ostrich knew she didn't stand a chance in the contest because of her bony neck and long skinny legs, so she sent Miz Coo-Coo Bird a bunch of the prettiest feathers you ever laid your eyes on.

The day for the contest came and all the birds were there. Miz Coo-Coo Bird was at the head of the parade and wasn't no two ways about it: She was the prettiest of them all. She was dressed in every color there was, and when all them colors blended together they created new colors what nobody had ever seen before and what nobody ain't never seen since.

The parade was scarcely a quarter over before Brer Rabbit stood up and waved his hand. "Stop the contest! Miz Coo-Coo Bird is the prettiest thing ever been put on the topside of the world."

The other birds had to go along with Brer Rabbit, and that was that. The band struck up the music for the dance they were going to have after the contest. Miz Coo-Coo Bird said they would have to excuse her, and she slipped through the bushes and was gone.

And ain't nobody seen her from that day to this. Well, maybe Brer Rabbit know where she is, but if he do, he ain't saying.

The other birds hunted high and low, low and high, sideways to sideways, up and down, and down and up. Everywhere they went, they hollered, "Coo-Coo! Coo-Coo!" That's what the Turtledove is doing when you hear it call. That's what the Pigeon is doing when you hear it. When the Rooster be making racket all through the night and day, he's calling and asking Miz Coo-Coo Bird to bring back the feather what he loaned her.

The old folks told me that when you see birds picking at their feathers and trying to straighten 'em out, what they're really doing is trying to see if the feather they loaned to Miz Coo-coo Bird has grown back.

Brer Fox and Uncle Mud Turtle

Uncle Mud Turtle was the oldest in the Turtle family. Some say he was so old that when the Lord created water and told it to be wet, the water come to Uncle Mud Turtle and asked him how to do that. So why Brer Fox think he could get the best of Uncle Mud Turtle is more than my mind can wrap around.

One day Brer Fox was down at the creek fishing. Maybe the fish heard that Brer Fox was coming, because he couldn't catch a cold.

It was getting over on the hindside of the day and Ol' Man Hungry was becoming good friends with Brer Fox. He put down his fishing pole and stuck his hand in the water. Maybe there was a big ol' catfish tucked in underneath the bank of the creek.

I don't know where the catfish were, but I do know where Uncle Mud Turtle was. He was laying under the bank sound asleep when he felt something fumbling around his head. He moved his head, but that didn't help.

Uncle Mud Turtle opened his mouth and the next time something felt around his head, he shut his mouth on it.

Brer Fox hollered so loud and so awful that folks ten miles away started crying. "Ouch! Turn me loose! Whatever you are, please turn me loose! Help! Help!"

Uncle Mud Turtle shut his mouth tighter until he felt comfortable. He was almost back to sleep when Brer Fox gave a holler so loud and a pull so hard that he jerked Uncle Mud Turtle out of the water.

When Uncle Mud Turtle got up on the bank and saw who he'd caught hold of, he opened his mouth and let Brer Fox go. "Excuse me, Brer Fox. I didn't know that was you. Hope I didn't do your hand no permanent harm. I'm truly sorry."

Brer Fox wasn't in the mood for no apologies. You know how it is. Sometimes we get our feelings hurt so bad that nothing will make 'em feel better until somebody else is hurting bad as we are. That ain't right, but that's just the way we be sometime.

Brer Fox's feelings were hurt because he hadn't been

able to catch nothing and the Hungries were walking back and forth across his stomach with spiked shoes on.

Uncle Mud Turtle saw how angry Brer Fox was, and he acted like he was scared. "Brer Fox, you got to believe me. If I'd known that was you, I would've kept my mouth shut. I know what a dangerous man you are. I knowed your daddy and your granddaddy, and you more dangerous than both of them put together."

"You right about that," answered Brer Fox. "And when I get through with you, the only place your folks will be able to find you will be in their dreams."

Uncle Mud Turtle cried on one side of his face and laughed on the other. "Please, Brer Fox, sir. Let me off this time. I promise I'll be your friend until Sister Moon catches King Sun."

Brer Fox wasn't hearing none of that and made a grab for Uncle Mud Turtle's neck. Uncle Mud Turtle pulled his head and his feet inside his shell.

Brer Fox was so hungry that he picked Uncle Mud Turtle up and started gnawing on the shell. He would've found something softer if he'd chewed on a rock.

From inside the shell Uncle Mud Turtle chuckled and said, "Brer Fox, hard ain't the name for my shell. You'll be jimber jawed before you gnaw through it."

Brer Fox keep on gnawing and gnawing and gouging and gouging.

This went on for a while and Uncle Mud Turtle was getting bored. All he wanted to do was get back under the bank and finish his nap. "Brer Fox, I'll tell you something. Teeth won't get my shell off. Claws won't get it off. But mud and water will." And with that Uncle Mud Turtle went back to sleep.

Brer Fox gnawed and gnawed and gouged and gouged until his mouth was sore and his teeth hurt. Uncle Mud Turtle was snoring so loud it sounded like a chain saw.

Brer Fox put him down on the ground and decided to play a trick on him. "Well, Uncle Mud Turtle, I got to get home and put some bandages on my hand. But you better believe that if it's the last thing I do, I'm gon' pay you back."

Brer Fox made a lot of racket like he was leaving. All he did was go hide behind some bushes. If he'd had any sense he would've known something that simpleminded wasn't gon' fool Uncle Mud Turtle.

Brer Fox's impatience got stirred up, and he came out from behind the bush and grabbed Uncle Mud Turtle. "You better tell me how to get your shell off, 'cause you know you can't outrun me."

"Teeth won't get it off. Claws won't get it off. Mud and water will do the work."

"I ain't got time for no riddles. Tell me how to get this shell off."

Brer Mud Turtle said, "Put me in the mud and rub my back as hard as you can, and the shell will come off."

Brer Fox took Uncle Mud Turtle over to a muddy place next to the creek, shoved him down in it, and started rubbing Uncle Mud Turtle's shell as hard as he could. The harder he rubbed, the deeper Uncle Mud Turtle sank into the mud until—bloop!—Uncle Mud Turtle disappeared.

Brer Fox felt around in the mud. Uncle Mud Turtle was gone. Before it occurred to Brer Fox that Uncle Mud Turtle was at home in the mud, which was how come he was named Uncle *Mud* Turtle, something grabbed Brer Fox's tale and dragged him into the water.

Brer Fox spluttered and kicked and splashed until he got back on dry land. He looked around and there was Uncle Mud Turtle floating in the water and laughing at him. Uncle Mud Turtle had sunk down through the mud and right into the creek.

That was one day Brer Fox would've saved himself a lot of time and trouble if he'd just gone to Wendy's for his dinner.

The Creature with No Claws

Sometimes folks ask me if these tales have any point to 'em, a moral, or something like that. I hope not! Nothing ruins a good story more than a commercial.

But that don't mean you can't learn nothing from these stories. What I've learned is not to believe what I see or what I hear, what I smell or what I taste. I believe only what I can put my hands on and feel. The truth is that folks fool themselves a lot worse than they get fooled by others. If you don't believe it, you ask Brer Wolf the next time you meet him in the big road.

Brer Wolf was going down the big road one day feeling mighty good. I don't know whether he'd just discovered a new mouthwash or what, but he was feeling like he was the boss of everything in the world and that included being able to tell Ol' Man North Wind when to blow, where to blow, and how strong. When somebody feels that good, they dangerous to the very person they want to protect the most—themselves!

Well, Brer Wolf was going down the road when he saw a track in the dirt. He stopped and looked at it.

"What kind of creature is this? Brer Dog didn't make that track. Brer Fox didn't make that track. Looks to me like it's a creature what ain't got no claws. I'm gon' follow him, and when I catch up to him, he'll be my meat!"

The track went up the road and down the road. It went off the road and on the road. It went straight and it went crooked. It zigged and it zagged, but Brer Wolf stayed right with it.

After a while the track started to look fresher and fresher. Brer Wolf stopped and examined it again. He still couldn't see no claw in it. He resumed following the track until, suddenly, he stopped dead still.

Right there in front of his eyes was the creature with no claws. It was the strangest-looking thing Brer Wolf had ever seen. It had a big head, sharp nose, and a bob tail and was walking around and around a big dogwood tree, rubbing his sides against it.

Brer Wolf said, "Looks to me like that creature been in a fight and lost most of his tail. And if that ain't bad enough, looks to me like that creature got some kind of itching disease, 'cause he's about to scratch all the bark off that tree."

Brer Wolf hollered, "Hey! You! What you scratching your hide on my tree for? If you ain't careful you gon' break it down."

The creature don't answer. He just keep on walking around and around the tree, scratching his sides and back.

"Didn't you hear me talking to you? Stop scratching your hide on my tree!"

The creature don't answer. He just keep on walking around and around the tree.

"You better answer me, you molly-dodger! Get out of my woods and leave my tree alone!"

Brer Wolf marched over to the creature like he was going to stomp him into the ground and make dust out of him. The creature kept on rubbing himself against the tree. You know how it is when you get an itch and you scratch and scratch and after a while it feels so good that you can't stop scratching? Well, that's how it was with the creature. He was just scratching and smiling, scratching and smiling. But when Brer Wolf got close, the creature stopped and stood up on his hind legs like a squirrel does when it's eating nuts.

Brer Wolf said, "Uh-huh. You begging, I see. Well, ain't gon' do you no good. I might've let you off if you had minded me when I hollered at you, but I got to teach you a lesson now so that next time I holler, you'll know I mean business."

The creature wrinkled up his face and mouth.

"Ain't no point in you scrunching up your face like you going to cry. Wait till I give you something to cry about."

Brer Wolf drew back his arm to hit the creature. The creature bopped Brer Wolf on the left side of his face, bopped him on the right side, and hit him square in the nose.

About four days later Brer Wolf woke up and wanted to know what had happened. His wife told him, "Fool, don't you know Brer Wildcat when you see him?"

Brer Polecat Finds a Winter Home

Late one year, 'long about the time when old Jack Frost was getting ready to come back from vacation and get to work, Brer Polecat knew it was time to find somewhere to stay for the winter.

He went and knocked on the door where Brer Rattlesnake was hiding from Jack Frost.

"Who's that?" Brer Rattlesnake say.

"It's me. Open the door."

"What you want?"

"It's getting kind of chilly out here," Brer Polecat answered.

"That's what I heard."

"It's too cold to stay out here. I might freeze to death."

"Do tell."

"Let me in there where it's warm."

Brer Rattlesnake say, "Two make a crowd, and I don't like crowds."

"I got a reputation for being a good housekeeper."

"So do I," said Brer Rattlesnake.

Brer Polecat was getting mad. "I'm gon' come in anyhow."

"Ain't room enough in here for both of us."

"I'll make room!" Brer Polecat hollered.

He backed off, got a running start, and slammed into the door. But Brer Rattlesnake had put a bar across the door. Every time Brer Polecat hit the door, it shook but it didn't fall. Wasn't nothing for Brer Polecat to do but go on his way.

Brer Bear had the biggest and warmest house of all the creatures. He had to, 'cause everybody in the Bear family was big and fat. They needed as much room as they could get.

The Bear Family was the happiest family too. There was the boy. His name was Simmon. The girl's name was Sue. And then there was Brer Bear, Miz Brune, and Miz Brindle. They all lived there in the house day after day and night after night. They ate their meals together and segashuated along from day to day, washing their face and hands in the same washpan and wiping on the same towel the way all happy families do.

One day when Jack Frost had put a hard layer of white on everything and Ol' Man North Wind was running around through the community making sure that everybody who wasn't indoors went there, there was a mighty knocking on Brer Bear's door.

"Who's knocking on my door at this time of year?" Brer Bear hollered.

Didn't no answer come, excepting that the banging got louder and bigger.

"Stop trying to tear down my door! Who you and what you want?"

"I'm one and therefore not two. If you are more than one, then who are you and what you doing in there?"

"What's your family name?" Brer Bear wanted to know.

"I'm the knocker and the mover, and if I can't climb over, I'll crawl under. Some call me Brer Polecat. Others call me a big word that ain't worthwhile remembering, but I want to move in. It's cold as the hair in a polar bear's nose out here, and something tells me that it's mighty warm in there where you are."

"It's warm enough for them what stays in here and don't go out there," said Brer Bear. "What do you want?"

"I want a lot of things what I don't get. But I'm a powerful housekeeper."

"I don't need no housekeeper, and there's just enough room for us what's already in here."

Brer Polecat said, "You might think you ain't got no room, but let me in and I'll make room, all the room I want."

Brer Bear opened the door and Brer Polecat came in. When Brer Polecat said he'd make room, he wasn't joking. His breath was so bad that Brer Bear and his whole family had to move out. And far as I know, Brer Polecat is still there.

Brer Bear and Brer Rabbit Take Care of Brer Fox and Brer Wolf

No matter how hard he tried, Brer Rabbit couldn't keep out of trouble. That seemed to be his nature. But when his head bought him trouble deeper than what he'd counted on, he called on his feet, because that's where he kept his lippity-clip and his blickety-blick.

One day Brer Rabbit decided to go bear hunting. You probably want to know how come something as little as Brer Rabbit would go hunting after something as big as Brer Bear. I don't know. But if there's one way to put gray hairs in your head, it's to worry with the ups and downs of Brer Rabbit. Now, maybe he had sense and maybe he didn't. Either way it don't make no difference, because the old times are gone forever, and if it wasn't for these tales, nobody would know that there'd ever been old times.

So, Brer Rabbit was going down the road and happened to meet up with Brer Fox and Brer Wolf. They said their howdy-dos and what all and sat down on the side of the road to tell all they knew and a lot more.

Brer Fox said he was bored. "Ain't nothing happening. No parties, no picnics, no barbecues."

Brer Wolf said he'd given up all that kind of stuff.

Brer Rabbit said, "I don't know what your problem is, Brer Fox. The only time I was bored was when I wasn't born. But even then I was kind of restless."

"Well, what you doing today to keep yourself entertained?"

"I'm getting ready to go bear hunting."

"Bear hunting!" exclaimed Brer Fox and Brer Wolf at

the same time. "You done lost your mind sho' 'nuf this
time, Brer Rabbit."

"Them's the very words my wife said just this very
morning. She said I'm gon' get myself killed."

Brer Wolf laughed. "She right about that. Something as
little as you can't catch no bear. I'm lots bigger than you,
but I'd think twice and dream four times before I went
out to hunt Brer Bear. Especially now. He just moved into
his brand-new house and he's still plenty mad about Brer
Polecat."

"That's the very reason why this is the best time to go
bear hunting. When a bear is mad, he can't think good."

Brer Fox and Brer Wolf let that roll around in their
brains for a minute and agreed that Brer Rabbit was right.

"My grandaddy's grandaddy said he'd had some bear meat
once and it was better than fried chicken with cranberry
sauce washed down with grape Kool-Aid."

"Do tell!" said Brer Wolf.

"I got a plan, but I need some help. Brer Wolf, if I get
Brer Bear on the run, will you and Brer Fox head him
off?"

Brer Wolf and Brer Fox looked at each other and nodded. "We'll do it, Brer Rabbit."

Brer Rabbit said he had to go make the arrangements
for the barbecue they would have after they caught Brer
Bear. "I'll meet y'all here same time tomorrow."

"Hold on, Brer Rabbit," said Brer Wolf. "Exactly what
is it that you want us to do? Don't get me wrong. I ain't
scared or nothing like that, but I just want to know what
the plan is."

"Don't worry about nothing. All you got to do is stand
your ground and not get scared when you see Brer Bear

coming. He'll be running faster than a locomotive on greased rails, but when he sees you, he'll turn to the side and I'll have him."

After Brer Rabbit left, Brer Wolf and Brer Fox looked at each other. "What you reckon he's really up to?" Brer Wolf wanted to know. "Brer Rabbit got more sense than to go hunting Brer Bear."

Brer Fox shook his head. "Beats me."

Brer Wolf smiled. "I bet I know. He's trying to make fools of us. He thinks we're scared. If we go tomorrow, he'll say that he can't find Brer Bear. If we don't go, he'll laugh and tell everybody that we were too scared."

Brer Fox smiled. "Well, if that's the case, I reckon we be obliged to show up."

While Brer Fox and Brer Wolf were wearing out their brains trying to figure out what Brer Rabbit was up to, Brer Rabbit was on his way to Brer Bear's house.

When he got there he didn't go up on the porch and knock on the door. He'd heard that Brer Bear was sitting behind his door with a shotgun and anybody who knocked on it was going to get blown halfway to Philly-Me-York.

Brer Rabbit stood out in the middle of the road and called out, "Hey! Brer Bear!"

After a few minutes Brer Rabbit heard the locks on the door being unfastened. That took about ten minutes, and then Brer Bear stepped out on the porch. "Come on in, Brer Rabbit!"

Brer Rabbit went in the house and him and Brer Bear sat down in the den. "Why don't we pop some popcorn, Brer Rabbit, and watch some videos. I just got some new ones. You seen the one called *The Brussels Sprout That Ate New York?*"

Brer Rabbit said he hadn't.

"I got another new one too, called *The Day Spinach Disappeared From the Face of the Earth*."

Seeing as how Brer Rabbit loved all kinds of greens, he said that sounded like a movie too scary for him to watch. "To tell the truth, Brer Bear, this ain't no pleasure visit. I got some important information I feel obliged to pass on to you."

"What's that?" Brer Bear wanted to know.

"I can't testify to the truth of it, you understand, but there's news going around the community that Brer Wolf and Brer Fox found some tracks in their cornfield, suspicious tracks."

"So? If I saw tracks in my field, I'd follow 'em to see where they led."

"Well, from what I hear, Brer Fox and Brer Wolf studied them tracks like detectives and decided that they'd be better off letting them tracks go on off by themselves. They figured that if they followed them tracks, they would end up in more trouble than they could handle."

"Nothing wrong with that. But you don't mean to tell me that Brer Wolf and Brer Fox gon' let the molly-dodger get away with something like that. There's more ways than one to deal with somebody like that."

"That's the truth, Brer Bear. Brer Wolf and Brer Fox done put out the word that they gon' have a big bear hunt. They sent engraved invitations to all the neighbors, at least all them that can read, and the neighbors are supposed to do the driving and they'll do the catching. They asked me if I wouldn't help with the driving, and I told 'em that I'd be more than happy to."

Brer Bear looked at Brer Rabbit real hard. "You told 'em that?"

"Sho' did. Told 'em that I'd help get you started running so they could catch you."

Brer Bear laughed, and his laugh sounded like thunder rolling the way it done when God told Noah to get in the ark. "Tell me something, Brer Rabbit," he asked when he stopped laughing. "How big a family Brer Wolf and Brer Fox got?"

Brer Rabbit shook his head. "Can't say as I know. We ain't been neighbors for a while. I moved off that block, 'cause I don't like them and they don't like me. And that's how come I came and told you what they was planning. Too, it seemed to me that this is something you'd probably like to take part in."

Brer Bear nodded. "I appreciate your thoughtfulness. Seems to me that I ain't got no choice but to be there."

Brer Rabbit and Brer Bear laughed and gave each other high fives and low fives and behind-the-back fives. Then they swapped tales and told jokes and laughed so much until Miz Brune and Miz Brindle came in the den and told Brer Rabbit that he better take his cottontail on home, 'cause all that laughing was keeping the children awake.

Brer Rabbit laughed all the way home and was still laughing when he got in bed.

Miz Rabbit poked her head out from under the covers. "What's wrong with you? What you been up to now?"

Brer Rabbit couldn't talk for laughing. Finally he caught his breath long enough to tell his wife what he was going to do. When she heard it, she didn't laugh one bit.

"You'll keep up with your foolishness until one of these days, somebody is going to catch you in your own trap and then I'll be a widow and have to go on welfare."

Brer Rabbit said, "There's been widows and orphans since the world started turning around." And with that he went to sleep. Miz Rabbit started thinking about filing divorce papers.

Next day Brer Rabbit met up with Brer Fox and Brer Wolf. "Let's go get some bear meat."

Brer Fox and Brer Wolf followed Brer Rabbit down the road and through the woods until they got to the place where the bushes are thick and the shadows are black.

Brer Rabbit stopped. He noticed that Brer Wolf and Brer Fox were hanging back. "You can't be bashful if you gon' help me catch Brer Bear."

Brer Fox and Brer Wolf came closer.

"That's perfect!" exclaimed Brer Rabbit. "Stand right there. I figure I'll have Brer Bear caught before he can get this far and if I do, I'll holler. But if he's too quick for me, I mean, if he gets the idea that I'm after him and starts running, I'll head him in this direction. All you two got to do is stand your ground."

Brer Fox and Brer Wolf stood their ground because they didn't want Brer Rabbit telling nobody afterward that they were afraid.

Brer Rabbit went to Brer Bear's house, which wasn't too far from there. They gave each other a whole bunch of high fives and low fives, and then Brer Bear took off running through the woods with Brer Rabbit close on his tail.

Brer Fox and Brer Wolf heard a loud and awful racket, and all of a sudden Brer Bear was coming straight toward them with Brer Rabbit close behind.

"Head him off!" Brer Rabbit hollered. "Head him off and hold him until I get there!"

Brer Bear was running so fast that blue smoke was rising off his body. Brer Fox and Brer Wolf held their ground

and Brer Bear kept coming. His head was down and his breath was hot and Brer Wolf and Brer Fox reached out to grab him.

Brer Bear hit Brer Wolf with his right hand and Brer Fox with his left. Brer Fox's eyeballs went to Chicago, his tail went to New York, and his hide found itself setting up on the beach in Miami. When Brer Wolf woke up three weeks later, he was speaking French. And Brer Rabbit? Shucks, he laughed so hard that his gray hair turned back to its rightful color.

Brer Fox Gets Away for Once

One summer there was an awful drought. I don't know if Ol' Rainmaker had gone on vacation or if he was on strike or what, but he wasn't on the job.

Every day it seemed like King Sun was angry from the time he got out of bed, 'cause his light was bright and hot. After a while the creeks and the streams started getting low. Pretty soon they dried up. The only water left was in a big lake.

Every day the animals met down at the lake to do their drinking. The big animals drank first, and by the time they finished drinking and stomping around in the water, it was too filthy for the little animals to drink.

They started looking lean and dry—all of them, that is, except Brer Rabbit. Didn't nobody know how he was getting water, but he was.

One day Brer Fox paid him a visit. "I got a problem, Brer Rabbit."

"Tell me about it. Problems are my meat."

"I'm thirsty. The big animals drink so much that by the time us little creatures get to the lake, ain't enough left for us to 'suage our thirst. What am I gon' do?"

Brer Rabbit thought for a little while. "Tell you what you do. Rub syrup all over yourself, and then roll around in some leaves. After that go down to the lake, and when the big animals come to drink, jump up in the air and shake yourself real hard. You'll look as scary as Ol' Boy, and the animals will run away. Then you can drink your fill."

Brer Fox did what Brer Rabbit had told him and went to the lake and hid.

It was close to sundown when the big animals came to drink. They were scuffling and hunching and pushing and scrounging to get as close to the water as they could. Brer Fox jumped out from behind a tree and yelled real loud, "Aaaargh!"

Brer Wolf was so scared he jumped over Brer Bear. Brer Bear was so scared he jumped over Brer Elephant. Brer Elephant decided it would take him too long to do any jumping, so he just started running and all the other creatures followed him.

Brer Fox chuckled and sauntered down to the lake, which he had all to himself. He was drinking his fill and didn't notice when the big creatures sneaked back to take another look at this strange monster. Brer Fox drank and drank, and being filled with all that water made him feel so good that he started playing in the water.

He was splashing around in the water and the syrup started to loosen. Before long all the leaves had washed off.

When the big creatures saw that the strange monster was none other than Brer Fox, Brer Bear yelled, "Let's get him!"

Brer Fox looked at himself and saw all the leaves had washed off, and he didn't waste no time getting away from there.

A day or two after that, Ol' Rainmaker came back from vacation or wherever he'd been, and all the creeks and streams got filled up again and the animals didn't have to worry about water no more.

Taily-po

Mr. Man should've had better sense than to mess with Brer Rabbit. So what if Brer Rabbit tried to eat up everything in Mr. Man's garden? Instead of getting mad Mr. Man should've been happy Brer Rabbit left him with a house to live in. The way Mr. Man acted, you would've thought he was the one who made the seed in his garden grow, and put the orange in the carrots and the red in the tomatoes.

One morning he woke up, looked out the window, and saw Brer Rabbit in his garden having broccoli for breakfast. That did it! Mr. Man called his hunting dogs, Ramboo, Bamboo, and Lamboo. "Go get Brer Rabbit and do away with him!"

When Brer Rabbit heard the dogs coming, he knew they weren't bringing him any hollandaise sauce to put on the broccoli, so he decided to get on away from there.

Round and round and up and down Brer Rabbit went, and round and round and up and down the dogs went. On one of them rounds, or it might've been on the up and down, the dogs started gaining on him.

Brer Rabbit headed for a big hollow tree down by the creek. When he got there, he ran inside, hurried up the stairs, and sat down in a rocking chair to catch his breath.

Now, don't come telling me there can't be stairs and a rocking chair in a hollow tree. Maybe there ain't such things in the hollow trees in your neighborhood. I don't know, 'cause I ain't never investigated the ones where you live. But where Brer Rabbit live, there was a tree with stairs in it and all sorts of other things too. I ain't gon' tell you what else was in the tree, 'cause you wouldn't believe me. I have to admit that I wasn't sure Brer Rabbit was telling the truth when he told me about the swimming pool in that tree, but I seen the rocking chair with my own three eyes.

Brer Rabbit was rocking in the rocking chair and Ramboo, Bamboo, and Lamboo were running around the tree with their noses to the ground trying to figure out which way Brer Rabbit went. They couldn't figure it out, though, and after a while they gave up and went home.

Brer Rabbit knew he had to do something or folks would be reading about him in the obituary column. There was only one thing he could do, and that was to go see Aunt Mammy-Bammy Big-Money.

She was the witch rabbit and she lived way off in a deep, dark, dank, smelly, slimy swamp. To get there you had to ride some, slide some, jump some, hump some, hop some, flop some, walk some, balk some, creep some, sleep some, fly some, cry some, follow some, holler some, wade some, spade some, and if you weren't careful, you still might not get there. Brer Rabbit made it, but he was plumb wore out when he did.

After he caught his breath, he hollered, "Mammy-Bammy Big-Money! Hey! Mammy-Bammy Big-Money! I journeyed far, I journeyed fast; I'm glad I found the place at last."

Big black smoke started belching up out of a hole in the

ground. The smoke got blacker and blacker until Brer Rabbit heard a voice that sounded like graveyard bones rubbing against each other: "Wherefore, Son Riley Rabbit Riley? Wherefore?"

"Mammy-Bammy Big-Money, Mr. Man is out to get me! If I don't do something, he's gon' make rabbit stew out of me."

Mammy-Bammy Big-Money made a terrible sound and sucked in all the black smoke and Brer Rabbit with it. He went tumbling down the hole, tail over head and head over tail, until, *blam!* He landed on the floor in Mammy-Bammy Big-Money's living room.

After his head cleared Brer Rabbit looked around. What he saw scared him so much that his ears lay down flat and didn't come up again for two months.

The walls of Mammy-Bammy Big-Money's house were made from tombstones. The long table she ate off of was made from bones, and at the head of the table was a chair made from skulls. Over in the corner was the bed she slept on and it was made from tiger's claws, and the pillow she laid her head on was a gorilla's skull. Brer Rabbit had never been one to do much praying, but he was praying in Latin and Hebrew and bebop that the Lord would let him get out of there alive!

Mammy-Bammy Big-Money didn't pay no attention to Brer Rabbit. She went over to the wall where an animal skin was hanging. It had a head, feet, and tails, but it wasn't the hide of any creature Brer Rabbit had ever heard about or seen on a *National Geographic* special.

Mammy-Bammy Big-Money took the skin off the wall and laid it on the floor. Then she sprinkled a handful of salt in the fire what was burning in the fireplace and sang:

Rise, skin, rise,
Open your big red eyes—
Sharpen your long black claws,
And work your big strong jaws!

As the salt started snapping and cracking in the fire, the animal skin began moving and stretching itself. Then it started rolling and wallowing around on the floor. When all the salt was burned, the animal skin rose up into a creature with a long tail.

It had been hanging on the wall so long that its hide was hard and stiff and it popped and screeched as the creature worked the wrinkles out. Before long it started feeling supple and was walking around and rubbing itself up against Mammy-Bammy Big-Money like a great big cat.

Mammy-Bammy Big-Money looked at Brer Rabbit and said, "Son Riley Rabbit Riley. Go. Rest in peace. Mr. Man will be taken care of."

Brer Rabbit was more than happy to get away from there. Everybody needs a relative like Mammy-Bammy Big-Money, but they ain't the kind you invite over to watch the Super Bowl with you.

That night, 'long about the time the ghosts in the graveyard were waking up, 'long about the time the full moon was peering in all the dark places and waking up the black cats, 'long about the time the witches were gassing up their brooms, Mr. Man was turning over for the second time and settling down into a deep and dreamless sleep.

Suddenly his eyes opened. "What was that noise?"

He listened.

He heard it again. Something was banging against the pots and pans in the kitchen.

Mr. Man got up and went to investigate.

By the light from the fire in the fireplace he saw a creature with a long tail. The creature saw Mr. Man and ran toward the door. Mr. Man hurried after it, and just as the creature was went out the door, Mr. Man grabbed its tail.

The tail came off in his hand!

Before Mr. Man could wonder about what kind of creature it was whose tail would come off, the tail started wriggling like it was alive. It was wriggling so hard, Mr. Man could hardly hold on to it.

He took it over to the fireplace and laid it on the hearth awhile. He put some wood on the fire to build it up. The tail was still wriggling, and the harder it wriggled, the bigger it got. It reared up and started hitting Mr. Man on his legs. Mr. Man grabbed the tail and threw it in the fire.

The tail started jumping about in the fire. Mr. Man grabbed the tongs and held the tail as tight as he could. It started sizzling like a piece of bacon frying.

After a while the tail stopped shaking and frying. Mr. Man didn't let go, however, until nothing was left but ashes.

Mr. Man went back to bed. He tossed and turned for a long time but finally he dozed off. Just as he got sleep good, there came a scratching and gnawing at the front door.

"Who's there?" he hollered out, sitting up straight.

It was quiet for a long time. Then a voice sang out:

> *Taily-po! You know and I know*
> *That I want my Taily-po!*
> *Over and under and through the door,*
> *I'm coming to get my Taily-po!*

Mr. Man called his dogs. "Here, Ramboo! Here, Bamboo! Lamboo—here, here! Here, dogs, here!"

The dogs came running. Mr. Man told them to go around the house and do away with whatever was scratching at the door. The dogs ran out and they took off running after something. In a minute they were out of hearing.

Mr. Man had just about dropped off to sleep again when there came a scratching and gnawing at the back door.

"Who's that?" he hollered, sitting up in bed.

After a little while a voice sang:

Your name, I know, is Whaley-Joe,
And before I'm going to really go,
I'd like to have my Taily-po;
Give me that and I'll gaily go—
Taily-po! My Taily-po!

Mr. Man went to the front door and called his dogs. The dogs don't answer and the dogs don't come. The gnawing and scratching at the back door is getting louder.

I know you know, and I know I know
That all I want is my Taily-po!

Mr. Man jumped in bed and pulled the covers over his head. He was shivering and quavering and didn't know what he was going to do.

The gnawing and scratching got louder and louder until, all of a sudden, it stopped. Mr. Man couldn't hear nothing. Then there came the sound of a creature's claws walking slowly across the kitchen floor.

The creature started throwing pots and pans around and breaking the dishes. Then it was silent again. Mr. Man was shaking and quavering so much that his bed started trembling.

Then he heard the creature scratching at something. The creature had smelled something in the fireplace and was scratching and pulling at the burning logs.

He scratched and he clawed and flaming coals and burning logs came flying out of the fireplace. They landed on the sofa and the curtains, and wherever they landed, a fire started.

The creature kept clawing and scratching until all the

fire was out of the fireplace and there, at the bottom, it found its tail, safe and sound. The creature grabbed the tail in its mouth and ran out of the house.

Mr. Man smelled smoke. He jumped out of bed and ran to the door of the bedroom and opened it. It seemed like the fire was standing there waiting for him, because as soon as he opened the door, the fire rushed into the bedroom like that was where it had been wanting to go the whole time.

Brer Rabbit was sitting in his rocking chair at home and said, "My goodness, I believe I smell smoke." He smiled.

And way off in the swamp Mammy-Bammy Big-Money raised her head, sniffed the air, and said, "I smell meat frying. I smell Mr. Man's meat frying."

Brer Rabbit, Brer Fox, and the Chickens

Once upon a time all the creatures ate meat. I better stop right here and tell you when "once upon a time" was.

"Once upon a time" was the time before time knew what it was supposed to be doing. Nowadays time has got a lot of flewjus mixed up with it. You think it's standing still, but it's callyhooting and humping and toting the mail. You can't hear the engine, but time has got one and it's a big one too, and time just be steady going. Don't come asking me where it's going. I don't think even time knows where it's going or much care. Its job is just to go and when it gets to where it's going, it just keeps on going. Some folks don't mind going along with time, and they can go right on. Time can let me stay right where I am now. But that's the funny thing about time. It don't leave nobody behind. I reckon that's how come I like these tales so much. They ain't inside time, and as long as I tell 'em, neither am I.

Now, like I was saying, once upon a time the creatures ate meat just like folks do. It was a sad day in the creature world when hay appeared on their dinner plates. Whenever you ever hear a creature howling in the nighttime, it's because that creature is remembering the rib-eye steaks and pork chops and barbecue it used to eat. Brer Rabbit was a filet-mignon-and-bernaise-sauce man and Brer Fox thought there was nothing better than spaghetti and meatballs.

The creatures loved meat so much that they wouldn't eat nothing else. After a while they had just about eaten all the meat in the country.

That wasn't good, especially for King Lion, who ate more meat than anybody. He was having a hard time keeping his big belly full, and if that wasn't bad enough, he got a thorn stuck in his foot and the only thing that could make him feel better was meat. So he issued a decree that all the creatures had to give him a share of their meat.

The meat may have made him feel better, but it didn't get the thorn out of his foot. After a while the pain got so bad that he had to send for the doctor. Guess who the doctor was? None other than Brer Rabbit himself!

Brer Rabbit wasn't like these doctors nowadays who stick needles in your behind and fill you full of pills and powders and pretty-colored liquids. Brer Rabbit got his medicines off the bushes and plants in the fields and woods. He knew that peach leaf was good for the bile and that sheep-sorrel salve was good for sores, and that white turpentine and mutton-suet would heal fresh hurts and cuts. I know y'all don't know what I'm talking about, but I can't be interrupting the story to be giving no medicine lessons. Just take my word for it.

Brer Rabbit wasn't none too happy about doctoring on King Lion. To get a good look at the foot the thorn was in, Brer Rabbit had to get close to King Lion's mouth, and King Lion's mouth was full of blood-red tongue and shiny, sharp teeth.

Every time Brer Rabbit felt King Lion's hot breath blowing on him, he got nervous, 'cause King Lion didn't always know how to control himself when fresh meat was close by. But he got the job done, put a salve on King Lion's foot to draw all the inflammation out, and then got on away from there.

When he walked out of King Lion's house, he noticed all the creatures waiting their turn to go in and give King Lion some meat. All the creatures were there, except Brer Fox.

"Where's Brer Fox?" Brer Rabbit asked.

Didn't nobody know.

"Anybody seen Brer Fox?" Brer Rabbit yelled.

The creatures shook their heads.

Brer Rabbit thought that was strange, but he went on down the road. As soon as he was out of sight of the creatures he sat down and started laughing. When his laughing fit was over, he continued on down the road.

He hadn't gone far when he saw somebody up ahead. It was Brer Fox. He was going toward his house with two fat chickens and Widdle-Waddle, the plumpest duck Brer Rabbit had ever seen.

Brer Rabbit hurried and caught up to him.

"Where you been?" Brer Rabbit asked. "I just come from

King Lion's and I didn't see you there. Everybody was asking about you. I told 'em you were feeling kind of feeble and were trying to put on some weight."

Brer Fox got nervous hearing that folks had been inquiring about him. "Did King Lion ask about me?" he asked anxiously.

"Sho' did. He called out your name more than once and more than twice. When he didn't get no answer, he put some language around your name that would burn a hole in my tongue if I repeated it. I hope King Lion is feeling better when you see him."

Brer Fox was real nervous now. "Did King Lion cuss?" he wanted to know.

"Well, let me put it to you this way. If you can think of something that's worse than cussing, then you getting close to what King Lion said about you."

"Have mercy, Brer Rabbit! What am I going to do?"

Brer Rabbit shook his head and said he didn't know. Brer Fox said he best be getting on down to King Lion's house.

Brer Rabbit snapped his fingers like he'd just remembered something important. He searched through his pockets and, with a sigh of relief, pulled out a piece of paper.

"Found it! After King Lion heated up the air talking about you, he give me this note and said I was to show it to you. He said you were supposed to tear off one corner and give it to him, and that'd be the proof that you'd seen it."

"Brer Rabbit? Is there any writing on that piece of paper? If there is, then it ain't gon' do me no good. I can read reading but I can't read writing."

Brer Rabbit said, "Well, that's how it is with me, except I can read writing but I can't read reading."

"Well, I see some writing on there. What does it say?"

Brer Rabbit looked at the piece of paper like he was trying to decipher what was on it. It wasn't nothing but a shopping list his wife had given him the week before, and it said, *half-gallon of milk, a pound of salami, a jar of mayonnaise, and a box of Godiva chocolate*. But Brer Rabbit scrunched up his nose, narrowed his eyes, and made like he was reading. "It say, *All and samely, whichever and whoever and wheresoever, especially the howcome and the what's-his-name, the aforesaid aforementioned and aftermentioned, let him come head first into the courthouse where the high sheriff and the law can lay him down and flatten him out, all whom this concerns, enough said.*"

Brer Fox scratched his head. "That don't sound good. What does it mean, Brer Rabbit?"

"It means that King Lion wants you to come up there where he can get his paws on you. You best get to King Lion's house quick as you can, Brer Fox. Tear off a piece of this note and show it to King Lion soon as you walk in."

Brer Fox moaned. "How am I going to get there in a hurry, Brer Rabbit? I got these two chickens and Widdle-Waddle. Maybe I better take them on home. I could get to King Lion's in no time if they weren't slowing me down. What do you think, Brer Rabbit?"

Brer Rabbit smiled. "I think that's a *good* idea."

Brer Fox headed for home and Brer Rabbit followed from a distance. He saw Brer Fox run in his house to put the chickens and Widdle-Waddle away, then hurry out again. Right behind him came his wife, hollering and yelling. "You better come back here and help me with these children of yours. I may have birthed them, but that don't mean they all mine. You act like I'm some kind of slave to you. I have to do every blessed thing there is to be done—split the wood, make the fire, do all the cooking, all the pulling and hauling, and on top of that, take care of your children. You just wait until I get to my consciousness-raising group next week."

She didn't really say that last part. That came out of my mouth when I wasn't looking.

Brer Fox didn't hear none of it 'cause he was steady moving down the road.

Brer Rabbit waited until Brer Fox was good and gone. Then he made his way up to Brer Fox's house.

He was walking slow, and the odor of politeness surrounded him like twenty-five-cent cologne. Anybody who didn't know better would've thought Brer Rabbit was a real gentleman. When Brer Rabbit acts like a gentleman, you better put your house under lock and key and call the FB and I for protection.

He walked on the porch and knocked softly on the door.

Miz Fox opened the door and Brer Rabbit, hat in hand, bowed low. "How you today, Miz Fox?"

"Don't ask, Brer Rabbit. What can I do for you?"

Brer Rabbit began to search in his pockets. "I got a note here for you, if I can lay my hands on it. Ah! Here it is!" He handed her the piece of paper.

Miz Fox took it and stared at it. "I ain't good at reading since these children broke my glasses. I don't know what I'm going to do, especially since my husband ain't got time to stay home and help me. When he does come in, it looks like the floor burns blisters in his feet and he's out the door again before I scarcely know he's been here. I tell you the truth, Brer Rabbit! If I'd known at first what I knew at last, I would've taken two long thinks and a mighty big thunk before I would've married anybody."

"Yes, ma'am," said Brer Rabbit. "Well, I met Brer Fox in the road just now. He asked me how I was doing, and I told him the truth. I said I had fallen on hard times, though it feel like hard times done fell on me. I'm a proud man and don't like to beg, I told him, but I don't have nothing to eat in my house. Everybody know that Brer Fox got a soft spot in his heart for the downtrodden, the oppressed, the impoverished, the tired, the poor, the weary, and them what's got bad feet. And he wiped his eye and say he couldn't stand it for me to be going around hungry."

"I wish he'd wipe his eye about some of my troubles," Miz Fox interjected.

"Yes, ma'am. Brer Fox say that just this very morning he had brought home two fat chickens and Widdle-Waddle Puddle Duck and he say I could have them. And he sat down and wrote it all out on that note I just gave you."

Miz Fox gave Brer Rabbit a hard look. Then she looked at the note again. She turned it upside down and round and round but she can't make out the letters without her glasses. "If this note ain't read until I read it, I feel sorry for the note. What does it say, Brer Rabbit?"

"Yes, ma'am." Brer Rabbit took the note and cleared his throat. *"To all whom it might contrive or concern, both now and presently: Be so pleased as to let Brer Rabbit have the chickens and Widdle-Waddle Puddle Duck. I'm well at this writing and hoping you are enjoying the same shower of blessings. The end."*

Miz Fox shrugged. "Well, it ain't no love letter." She went in the back and brought the two chickens and Widdle-Waddle and gave them to Brer Rabbit.

"Blessings on you," Brer Rabbit said. He went home and didn't waste no time getting there. He told his wife to cook the chickens and Widdle-Waddle Puddle Duck like they was having company for dinner, and then he hurried back to see after King Lion's foot.

When he got to King Lion's house, Brer Fox was waiting outside for his turn to go in. Brer Fox had the really-truly goodness dripping from his mouth and oozing from his hide. He looked like what folks used to call " 'umble-come-tumble." He was scared that King Lion was going to do away with him, so when he saw Brer Rabbit, he was relieved.

"Brer Rabbit! Brer Rabbit!"

"I'm mighty glad to see you, Brer Fox. After we talked, I got scared that you would go in and see King Lion without me, and that would've been mighty bad for you."

"I was going to go in like you told me to, but the other creatures told me to get in line and wait my turn. I'm sho' glad to see you."

"Well, Brer Fox, you stay right here and don't try to go in there where the King is until I give you the word. I don't know what he might do to you."

Since Brer Rabbit was the doctor, he could go in to see the King anytime, so he elbowed his way through the creatures and walked into King Lion's throne room.

King Lion's paw was wrapped up like Brer Rabbit had left it, and King Lion was just dropping off to sleep. He started snoring like he'd swallowed a horse—mane and hoof. Brer Rabbit went back out.

"What's the news?" Brer Fox wanted to know.

Brer Rabbit put his arm around Brer Fox's shoulder. "You better get out of here. King Lion is terribly upset at how you been acting. I begged for you, Brer Fox. I begged and begged. Finally King Lion said he'd let you off this time, but the next time, have mercy on you! You best go on home, Brer Fox, before your wife gives away them fat chickens and Widdle-Waddle."

Brer Fox laughed. "I'd like to see somebody get them chickens and Widdle-Waddle away from my wife. You a smart man, Brer Rabbit, and if you can get them chickens and that duck away from my wife, you're welcome to them."

Brer Rabbit bowed low. "I sho' do thank you, Brer Fox. I sho' do thank you." And he went lippity-clippiting down the road, laughing so loud that all the trees wanted to know what the joke was.

Brer Fox Tries to Get Revenge

You probably won't believe this, but there be some folks that wouldn't enjoy that tale I just told. Somebody come telling me once that it was a story about stealing and that Brer Rabbit wasn't nothing but a liar and a thief and a scoundrel. Them words hurt me in the heart so bad I had to eat a gallon of Häagen-Dazs coffee ice cream before I started feeling better.

It ain't possible to be friends with these stories without shaking off a lot of your ideas. No doubt about it. You have to shuck them ideas like you shucking corn.

Folks got their laws and the creatures got theirs, and that's just how it is. But folks have the notion that everybody got to think like they do. Like the time I painted my house yellow. Folks come around saying, how come you paint your house yellow when everybody else's house is painted white? Well, I didn't want to live in a white house. I see the color white and it makes me think of snow and ice, and what I want to be sitting up in my house shivering in the middle of summer? So I painted my house yellow, and in the winter I be sitting inside, and that yellow color on the outside make me feel all warm and cozy.

But most folks get upset if you don't think the way they do. If they had different eyes, and if their eyes were on a different level, they wouldn't see the way they do, and consequently they wouldn't think the same way either. Take Brer Turtle, for example. He looks on the world from both sides of his head. That's how come can't nobody get the best of him. He see trouble coming from the east and the west at the same time. But you and me have to turn our heads to see trouble coming from the east and while we looking east, trouble from the west done come and grabbed us and is carrying us on down the road. So that's how come creature laws ain't folks' laws.

To all them what think Brer Rabbit was a thief, well, there's clearly some things they ain't thought about. In the first place, why would anyone think that them chickens and that duck belonged to Brer Fox? From what I know about Brer Fox, that ain't very likely. On top of that, we know he didn't get them at home, 'cause that's where he was headed. He didn't get them in the woods, 'cause chickens and puddle ducks don't grow on trees, and if they did, Brer Fox can't climb no higher than he can jump. Now, you can put it down and carry four, that wherever Brer Fox laid his hands on them, he didn't buy them, and neither were they given to him. You don't have to guess about that; you know it by your nose and your two big toes.

And another thing. Them chickens and duck probably didn't belong to the one Brer Fox tuck them from. It would take a long time to hunt up and search out the nicknames and pedigrees of all who had them chickens and duck before they came into Brer Rabbit's hands.

Now, the reason I go into such a long explanation is not because I done decided to run for president but because this is what you call a two-horse tale. But just like you can't hitch two horses to a wagon at the same time, you got to tell one tale at a time. So, let me get the other horse hitched up.

Brer Rabbit and Brer Fox were outside King Lion's, and Brer Fox told Brer Rabbit that if anybody could get them chickens and Widdle-Waddle Paddle Duck from his wife, they could have 'em.

Brer Rabbit laughed so hard that the rocks in the ground wanted to know what the joke was. (Folks don't realize it, but there ain't nothing in nature enjoy a good joke more than a rock. You don't know what laughing is until you've heard a rock laugh.)

Brer Fox went on home. Brer Rabbit decided to follow to see what was going to happen when Brer Fox found out that his chickens and Widdle-Waddle Puddle Duck were gone.

Brer Fox walked in the door, and he could tell by the way his wife was standing at the stove that she was mad at him. "What's the matter, sugar-honey?" he asked.

"I'll sugar you! I'll honey you! How come you brought food home for us and the children to eat and then have me give it away? It don't make no sense for you to carry two fat chickens and a duck home and then five minutes later give them away. And how come you want to give them to Miz Rabbit? What is she to you, anyhow? I'm sitting up here just dribbling at the mouth thinking about how good them chickens and that duck going to taste and here come Brer Rabbit, bowing and scrapping and simpering and sniggering and grinning, saying you'd sent him to get the chickens and duck. He never would've gotten them from me if he hadn't had that note what you wrote, and you know good and well that since the children broke my glasses and you been too trifling to buy me new ones, I can't read *B* from *bull's foot*."

Brer Fox didn't know what she was talking about. "I didn't write you no note," he said. "Sugar-honey, dumpling-pie, ain't we been married long enough for you to know that I can't write writing?"

"I been married to you long enough to know I made a mistake. If I'd married Brer Mink like he wanted me to, at least I would've had a coat when he died. All I want to know is how come you giving our food away to Brer Rabbit and his family? Your own children done got so skinny they can't make a shadow in the moonshine. And if you got to give away our food, why give it to the Rabbit family? You know as well as I do that I don't like to associate with folks who got big eyes. Folks with round eyes ain't got too much intelligence. Plus, they smell bad."

Brer Fox didn't know what she was talking about, but the idea had gotten through to him that the chickens and Widdle-Waddle Paddle Duck were gone.

"Woman, put the brakes on your lips and park your mouth on the side of the road. Do you mean to stand there, flat footed and right before my face and eyes, and tell me that you took them fat chickens that I brought home, and that juicy Widdle-Waddle Paddle Duck, which I also brought home, and give them to Brer Rabbit for no reason?"

"You sent me a note and that's what the note say."

"Let me get this straight. You ain't got no more sense than to believe something that's written on a piece of paper? How come you didn't ask Reginald the Fourth to read that piece of paper? He in college and he can read reading and writing in fourteen languages."

Miz Fox got mad at Brer Rabbit now. She swore that when she saw him she was going to put a hurting on him so bad that the Devil would ask her to have mercy.

Brer Rabbit was hiding alongside the house and he started laughing. He laughed so hard and so loud that Brer Fox heard him.

"I'm going to get some rabbit meat to make up for the chicken meat you gave away. You go out on the porch and be sweeping in front of the door. You pretend like you talking to me inside the house. I'll slip out the back and sneak up on Brer Rabbit."

Miz Fox went on the porch and started sweeping and talking. "You better get on up from there and go out and get us something to eat instead of trying to think up on how you gon' get revenge on Brer Rabbit. Revenge can wait. Hungriness can't."

Miz Fox was sweeping and talking, and she didn't see Brer Rabbit until he was right there on the porch with her.

"How do, Miz Fox," he said politely. "I hope you well this evening."

Miz Fox jumped but figured she'd get Brer Rabbit in a conversation so Brer Fox could catch him. "I ain't doing too well, Brer Rabbit. My husband done come down with lumbago of the brain and ain't feeling too well."

"I'm sorry to hear that. I been going around through the community this evening and seems like almost everybody is laid up there. Folks say that a plate of lasagna and wintergreen LifeSavers will clear it right up." Brer Rabbit looked at Miz Fox strangely.

"What you looking at me for like you crazy?"

"I beg your pardon, Miz Fox. I was just wondering how come you ain't got on your new dress."

"New dress? What you talking about?"

"The one made out of calico what King Lion gave to Brer Fox to give to you!"

Miz Fox laid the broom down. "You mean the King sent me a dress? I ain't never laid one eye or the other on it."

Brer Rabbit acted like he was embarrassed. "You'll have to excuse me, ma'am. I believe I done put my mouth where it didn't have no business being. I never like to come between a husband and wife, not me! But Brer Fox is right there in the house. Ask him yourself."

Miz Fox was so mad about not getting the dress and wondering who Brer Fox had given it to that she didn't care what she said. "He ain't in the house. He's sneaking around the house to grab you for taking the chickens and Widdle-Waddle Paddle Duck."

Brer Rabbit laughed. "That Brer Fox is quite a man. That he is. Now, that's the way you see it, Miz Fox. The way I see it is that Brer Fox saw me coming and is hiding out 'cause he was afraid I was going to ask you about that calico dress King Lion sent you. It was a pretty dress too, and if I'd knowed then what I know now, I would've gotten that dress from Brer Fox to give to my wife. That's just what I would've done!"

Brer Rabbit bowed and made his farewells and went and hid in some bushes.

He wasn't a minute too soon, because here come Brer Fox from around the side of the house. "Where is that molly-dodger? He was right here. I know he was. Where'd he go?"

Before Brer Fox could say another word, Miz Fox was going all upside his head with the broom. Brer Fox thought he'd been hit by lightning. He fell down on the ground and started rolling over and over, but Miz Fox's aim was deadly and whichever way he rolled, Miz Fox was right there with the broom.

Eventually the broom wore out and when the dust cleared, Brer Fox got an idea of what had hit him. "Honey! What's the matter with you? What you hitting me for? I ain't Brer Rabbit. Whatever it is, I swear to you I ain't gon' do it no more!"

"So, it's true, is it?" Miz Fox yelled and she started in on him again. Since there wasn't much broom left, she hit him with the handle.

Finally the broom handle wasn't nothing but splinters. Miz Fox had run out of breath and Brer Fox had run out of bones to break. They both just flopped down in the dust.

Then Miz Fox started crying, and that was worse for Brer Fox than the beating. That's the truth. I done seen men who could kill a herd of tigers with their bare hands be totally helpless before a crying woman.

"How come you didn't give me that calico dress King Lion give to you to give to me?" she asked him finally, sniffing and bawling.

"What calico dress? I didn't get to see King Lion today."

"But you said you wasn't going to do it no more."

"I said that to try to get you from stop beating on me."

They looked at each other and realized that Brer Rabbit

had tricked them again. They decided that if it was the last thing they did, they were going to do away with that rabbit.

For the next two weeks everyplace Brer Rabbit went, Brer Fox or Miz Fox was right with him. Brer Rabbit thought this was fun, but after a while it started to get boring. Not only that, Brer Rabbit was afraid that his luck might run out just when he needed it the most and he'd be caught.

Along about that same time King Lion sent word that he wanted to see Brer Rabbit. The place on King Lion's foot where the thorn had been had swollen up into a great big blister and it hurt so bad that the King couldn't sleep.

Brer Rabbit went straight to the place where King Lion done his kinging, and it didn't take him long to get there. When Brer Rabbit takes a notion to go somewhere right quick, he just picks up the miles with his feet and drops them off again like a dog shedding fleas.

Brer Rabbit took one look at King Lion's foot and shook his head. "King, this foot of yours is sho' 'nuf in a bad way."

"What can I do about it?" King Lion wanted to know.

"Ain't but one cure for a foot that done swole up this bad."

"What is it?"

Brer Rabbit said, "Well, it's a cure I don't like to prescribe, and if you wasn't the King, I wouldn't prescribe it. But we can't have a King with a sore foot. Ain't no two ways about that. There's only one thing that will make your foot well. You have to wrap your foot in fox hide. And not only that. The hide must be so fresh that it's warm."

Brer Rabbit started crying. "Po' Brer Fox! I'm sho' gon' miss him. Me and him done had some good times on the topside of the world. That's the truth!" He sniffed and wiped his eyes. "King, I'd appreciate it if you'd let me slip on out the back door before you do what you got to do to Brer Fox. I'll just go on off in the woods yonder and wonder at the flight of time and the changes the years bring."

He bowed to the King. "Next time I see you your foot will be well. But what will Brer Fox be?"

King Lion said, "He'll be nothing but a hide. You want me to send you his hide?"

Brer Rabbit said, "No, please don't. I couldn't bear to look at it. Just send it to Miz Fox. It might be some sort of comfort to her in her grief."

King Lion's foot got well; Brer Fox got dead, and Brer Rabbit? Shucks. Brer Rabbit got away.

———————

Brer Wolf and the Pigs

Everybody knows the story of the three little pigs. Well, that story ain't right. It might be right for whoever tells it and don't know no better, but I know better. Anybody who believe that story is getting shortchanged, 'cause there're only three pigs in that story. In the *real* story, the one I'm about to tell you, there are five pigs.

If memory serves me right, there was Big Pig, then come Little Pig, and after that was Speckle Pig, and then Blunt, and last and lonesomest was Runt.

These pigs had a rough time. Their daddy died while they was still little, and they'd just gotten to the age where they could halfway take care of themselves when their mama came down terrible sick, and she knew she wasn't gon' get better.

She called all her children in and told them she wasn't gon' be in the world much longer. "You going to have to look out for yourselves. You'll get along fine if you always keep a lookout for Brer Wolf. As long as you live, beware of Brer Wolf!"

Big Pig, she said she wasn't scared of Brer Wolf. Little Pig say, she ain't either. Speckle Pig put her penny in the pot and say she wasn't scared. Blunt say he almost as big as Brer Wolf, so he wasn't scared. Runt, she don't say nothing but just grunt.

Not long after that, Miz Pig died, and the children were on their own.

Big Pig, she went and built her a house out of brush. Little Pig, she built a stick house. Speckle Pig, she built a mud house. Blunt built himself a plank house. Runt went to work and built herself a stone house.

Well, one morning here come Brer Wolf, licking his chops and shaking his tail.

First house he came to was Big Pig's. Brer Wolf knocked politely on the door—*knock, knock, knock.* Nobody answered.

Brer Wolf never was one to waste time on being polite, and this time his knock had some sense in it—*blam! blam! blam!*

That got Big Pig's attention. "Who's that?"

"A friend," said Brer Wolf. And then he sang:

*If you'll open the door and let me in
I'll warm my hands and go home again.*

Big Pig wasn't too big on music, so she said again, "Who's that?"

"How's your mother?" Brer Wolf wanted to know.

"My mother's dead," answered Big Pig, "and before she died she told me to keep on the lookout for Brer Wolf. You sound mighty like Brer Wolf to me."

Brer Wolf sighed. "I don't know why your mama would say something like that. I heard that Miss Pig was sick and I decided I'd bring her some corn. If your mama was here right now and feeling like herself, she'd take this corn I done brought and be mighty thankful. She'd ask me in so I would warm my hands by the fire."

The thought of the corn made Big Pig's mouth water so, she opened the door and let Brer Wolf in. That was the last anybody ever saw of Big Pig. Brer Wolf didn't give her time to squeal or to grunt before he gobbled her up and swallowed her down.

The next day Brer Wolf played the same trick on Little

Pig. He banged on her door and sang his song. Little Pig let him in. He returned the favor and let Little Pig into his stomach.

A few days later Brer Wolf paid a call on Speckle Pig. He banged on her door and sang his song. But Speckle Pig was suspicious and wouldn't open the door.

Brer Wolf started some sweet talk then. "How come you treating me this way? It's as cold as the hairs in a polar bear's nose out here. At least let me stick one of my paws inside so it can get warm."

Speckle Pig opened the door a crack and Brer Wolf stuck his paw inside. "That sho' feels good. But having this paw warm makes the other paw feel even colder. Please, could I stick it in too?"

Speckle Pig opened the door a little bit more. Well, no need to drag this out. Brer Wolf kept pleading until he had his whole body in the house, and that was the last anybody ever heard of Speckle Pig.

The next day Brer Wolf made a meal out of Blunt. Wasn't nobody left now but Runt. And that's where Brer Wolf should've left well enough alone. He would've been a smart man if he hadn't been too smart.

Runt was the littlest of the pigs, but she had so much sense that it was a bother to her sometimes.

Brer Wolf banged on Runt's door and sang his song:

> *If you'll open the door and let me in,*
> *I'll warm my hands and go home again.*

Runt had more sense than to believe something like that. Brer Wolf talked sweet, but Runt didn't listen sweet. Finally Brer Wolf decided to break the house in, but he

took a long look at that stone and knew that wouldn't work.

Brer Wolf decided to pretend that he'd gone home, and he went off and laid in the shade for a while.

Then he came back and knocked at the door—*blam! blam! blam!*

"Who's that?" asked Runt.

"It's Speckle Pig," said Brer Wolf. "I brought you some peas."

Runt laughed. "My sister, Speckle Pig, never talked through that many teeth."

Brer Wolf went away again and laid in the shade for a while more.

Blam! blam! blam!

"Who's that?" Runt wanted to know.

"Big Pig," said Brer Wolf, "I brought you some corn."

Runt looked through a crack in the door. "My sister never had hair on her foot."

That did it! Brer Wolf was mad now.

"I'm coming down the chimney!" he hollered.

"Come on," Runt told him.

When Runt heard Brer Wolf on the roof, she grabbed an armful of straw. When Brer Wolf started down the chimney, she put the straw on the fire. The smoke from that straw was thick. It got in his throat and in his eyes, and he was coughing so hard and his eyes were watering so much that he lost his balance and fell right smack into the fire. And that was the end of Brer Wolf.

At least that was the end of *that* Brer Wolf.

Mr. Benjamin Ram and His Wonderful Fiddle

Mr. Benjamin Ram was the nicest of all the animals. That's probably because he was a musicianer. He was an old-time fiddle player. What I mean is that he patted his foot while he played. If a fiddle player pats his foot while he's playing, he's playing that old-timey music, the kind that can turn white milk into yellow butter.

Mr. Benjamin Ram lived way back out in the woods, but he didn't get to spend much time at home, 'cause whenever the creatures wanted to have a party, and that was near about every weekend, they wanted Mr. Benjamin Ram and his fiddle.

He'd sit there in a chair, put the fiddle under his chin, close his eyes, and get to bowing and patting his foot, and next thing the animals knew, they'd be dancing as good as Baryshnikov and Sandman Sims rolled into one. When the party was over, the creatures would fill up a big bag of peas for Mr. Benjamin Ram to carry home with him.

One time Miz Meadows and Miz Motts and the girls decided to have a party. I don't know what they was celebrating. If my recollections serve me right, it was the birthday of toenail polish. Whatever it was, they got word to Mr. Benjamin Ram that they expected him to be there with his fiddle.

The day of the party came, but King Sun didn't come up that morning. The clouds were spread out all across the elements and the wind started to blow cold. That didn't matter to Mr. Benjamin Ram. He took down his walking cane and put his fiddle in a bag and set out for Miz Meadows's place.

He thought he knew the way, but the wind started blowing colder and colder and the clouds got thicker and darker, and before Mr. Benjamin Ram knew it, he was lost.

If he'd stayed on the big road, he would've gotten there without any problem, but he had tried to take a shortcut. Sometimes what seems like the short way turns out to be the wrong way and the long way. That's how it turned out with Mr. Benjamin Ram.

The minute he realized he was lost, he tried to find himself. He went this way and that way and the other way, and they was all the wrong way. Some folks would've sat right down where they were and studied on the situation, but Mr. Benjamin Ram's other name was Billy Hardhead, and thinking was not an activity he ever took much time out for. Other folks would've started bawling and calling until they woke up everybody in the county. Mr. Benjamin Ram kept on trying to find the way out and kept getting farther and farther in.

The sky turned dark like it was nighttime, and Mr. Benjamin Ram began to feel lonesome. After a while Ol' Man Night dropped down and Mr. Benjamin Ram knew he was going to have to sleep in the woods.

Just about that time he came up over a hill and down at the bottom, in the valley, he saw a light. He took foot in hand and hurried toward that light like it was the very place he'd been looking for.

Before long he came to the house where the light was and knocked on the door.

"Who's that?" came a voice from inside.

"I'm Mr. Benjamin Ram and I done lost my way. Could you take me in for the night?"

"Come in," said the voice from the other side of the door.

Mr. Benjamin Ram walked in, shut the door behind him, and bowed politely. Then he looked around and he began shaking and quivering like he'd come down with the Florida flu. Sitting there in front of the fireplace was none other than Brer Wolf, and his teeth were showing all white and shiny and sharp like he'd just polished them with car wax.

Mr. Benjamin Ram wanted to put himself in reverse and get away from there, but Brer Wolf jumped up and barred and fastened the door.

Mr. Benjamin Ram was in a mess of trouble, but he decided to act like nothing was wrong. "It's good to see you, Brer Wolf. How you and your family been?"

"Very well," answered Brer Wolf.

"Glad to hear it. I appreciate you letting me come in to warm myself by your fire. I'd appreciate it even more if you'd point me in the direction of Miz Meadows's house. Seem like I made a wrong turn somewhere and went left when I should've gone right, or went right when I should've gone left."

"Be happy to," says Brer Wolf. "But why don't you put your walking cane and fiddle down and make yourself at home. We ain't got much, but what we got is yours. We'll take good care of you." Brer Wolf laughed a wolfy laugh and his teeth were gleaming like knives.

Mr. Benjamin Ram started shivering and shaking again like he was coming down with the New Orleans pneumonia.

Brer Wolf slipped into the back room and while Mr. Benjamin Ram was sitting in front of the fire thinking he had caught the Chicago chilblains, he heard Brer Wolf whispering to his wife:

"Ol' woman! Ol' woman! Throw away the smoked meat. We got fresh meat for supper."

Mr. Benjamin Ram heard Miz Wolf sharpening a knife on a rock—*shirrah! shirrah! shirrah!*—and every *shirrah* was bringing him that much closer to the cooking pot.

Mr. Benjamin Ram knew that the end was near, so he decided he might as well play his fiddle one last time.

He took it out of the bag and tuned it up—*plink, plank, plunk, plink, plink, plank, plunk!*

When Miss Wolf heard the sound, she didn't know what it was. "What's that?" she asked Brer Wolf.

They cocked their ears to listen, and just about that time Mr. Benjamin Ram put the fiddle under his chin, got his bow, and started playing one of them old-time tunes. I believe the one he played was "I'm as Good Looking as a Rat in a Tuxedo." Then again, it might've been "Don't Cry for Me, Argentina." I don't rightly remember.

Whatever it was, he was sho' 'nuf playing it. He had his eyes closed and his foot was going, and to tell the truth he didn't know where he was anymore. When Mr. Benjamin Ram got to playing, he forgot everything except the music. That's how come he was so good.

Brer Wolf hadn't heard music like that in all his days. It seemed like the notes of the music were bouncing up and down on his hide and beating on his eyeballs and pulling at his ears, and the faster Mr. Benjamin Ram played, the more the notes of music bounced and beat on Brer Wolf. He couldn't take it no more, and he lit out through the back door and headed for the swamp, Miz Wolf right with him.

After a while Mr. Benjamin Ram stopped playing. He looked around and didn't see Brer Wolf. He listened and he didn't hear Miz Wolf. He looked in the back room. Nobody there. He looked on the back porch. Nobody there. He looked in the closet. Nobody there.

Mr. Benjamin Ram locked all the doors, fixed himself some supper, then lay down in front of the fire and went to sleep.

Next morning when he got up, it was bright and sunny and he didn't have no trouble finding his way to Miz Meadows's house.

When he got there he apologized for not making it to the party the night before. Miz Meadows say they couldn't have no party without him. But that wasn't the truth. Brer Rabbit had gone home and gotten his saxophone and them

creatures had just stopped partying about a half hour before Mr. Benjamin Ram got there. But didn't nobody tell
him, 'cause they didn't want to hurt his feelings.

Mr. Benjamin Ram Triumphs Again

Mr. Benjamin Ram was old, but that don't mean he wasn't
vigorous. He was a sight to see, with his wrinkly horns,
shaggy hair on his neck, and red eyes. And when he shook
his head and snorted and pawed his feet, he looked almost
as fierce as Ol' Boy.

One day Brer Fox and Brer Wolf were coming down
the road and Brer Fox said, "I'm hungry in the neighborhood of my stomach."

Brer Wolf was astonished. "How can you be hungry
when Mr. Benjamin Ram be laying up in his house just
rolling in fat?" Seems like Brer Wolf had forgotten that he
had had Mr. Benjamin Ram in his house and hadn't gotten none of that fat.

Brer Fox shook his head. "I look at Mr. Benjamin Ram
and I lose my appetite."

Brer Wolf laughed. "What kind of man are you? How
can you lose your appetite when Mr. Benjamin Ram rolling in fat like he ain't never heard of skinny?"

Brer Fox gave Brer Wolf a hard look. "I hear tell that
you tried to get Mr. Benjamin Ram in the pot and you
ended up sleeping in the swamp."

Brer Wolf's mouth started moving like he wanted to say
something, but when truth slap you in the mouth, first

thing you better do is be sure you still got all your teeth.

Brer Fox chuckled. "You right, Brer Wolf. Mr. Benjamin Ram is just rolling in fat and I'm hungry. Let's get us some of that fat."

Brer Wolf's jaw fell. "Well, to be honest with you, Brer Fox, I just remembered that today is the day I'm supposed to be the judge at a sneaker-smelling contest."

"This ain't gon' take long. We close to his house as it is."

Brer Wolf went on with Brer Fox. Before long they were knocking on Mr. Benjamin Ram's door. They were expecting the door to open, but Mr. Benjamin Ram came from around the side of the house.

They looked around and there he was, staring at them with his red eye. Brer Wolf jumped up in the air and started running before his feet touched the ground. When he realized what he was doing, he stopped and came back, 'cause he didn't want Brer Fox telling all the creatures that he'd gotten scared and run away.

Brer Fox laughed and laughed. "You may be puny in the mind, Brer Wolf, but you are definitely feeling good in your legs."

Mr. Benjamin Ram went and sat on the porch. "Brer Fox! I thank you for bringing Brer Wolf to me. I just about done run out of meat. My wife was telling me this morning that the freezer is almost empty. I'll just chop and pickle Brer Wolf, and that'll hold me and my family for a few months. We ain't had no wolf meat in a long time."

Brer Wolf didn't need to hear nothing else. Neither did Brer Fox. They ran away from there so fast that the wind they created almost knocked Mr. Benjamin Ram's house down.

That was one time when Mr. Benjamin Ram made the acquaintance of his brain. I wonder if he'd been talking with Brer Rabbit.

How the Bear Nursed the Alligators

Once there was a Bear who lived in the swamp in a hollow tree. She had two little bears and she loved her children more than honey.

Every morning she went out bright and early to find food for them. One day she was gone for a long time and the two children got very hungry. The little boy Bear said to his sister, "I'm tired of waiting for Mama. I'm going down to the creek and catch some fish."

The little girl Bear looked scared. "Mama said something might catch us if we go out. You better mind what Mama says."

The little boy Bear laughed. "Hush up! And don't tell mama either."

He climbed out of the tree and went down to the creek.

He was standing on the bank of the creek when a big log came floating toward him. "That's the very thing I need. I'll stand on that log and catch some fish from there."

The little boy Bear jumped on the log. As soon as he did, the log turned around and started toward the middle of the creek.

"What kind of log is this?" the little boy Bear wondered. He looked at the log more closely and what he saw made

him tremble all over. It wasn't a log. It was a great big Alligator!

The Alligator flicked her tail and hit the little boy Bear in the back. Then she turned around and opened her mouth wide so that he could see all of her teeth.

"I've been hunting breakfast for my children, and I believe I found it," said the Alligator.

The Alligator swam to her hole in the bank and slithered inside, the little boy Bear on her back.

"Children! Come see what I brought you for breakfast!" shouted the Alligator.

She had seven children. They were lying in the bed, and when they heard their mama mention breakfast, they raised up and opened their mouths.

The little boy Bear took one look at those baby alligators and all their tiny sharp teeth, and he started crying. "Please, Miz Alligator. Give me a chance to show you what a good nurse I am. I know you must worry about your children when you're out hunting food for them. I'll mind the children for you and take some of the worriment out of your gray matter."

The Alligator thought for a moment and decided that wasn't a bad idea. "I'll try you for one day," Miz Alligator said. "If you any good, I'll try you again tomorrow. If you not, we'll eat you today."

"I'm good! I'm good!" said the little boy Bear.

Miz Alligator left.

The little boy Bear sat down. After a while he started to get hungry. His stomach growled. Even a baby bear's growling stomach sounded like a thunderstorm was coming.

Time passed. His stomach growled louder. More time passed. The little boy Bear was so hungry he could hardly hold up his head.

"Ain't no way I'm gon' starve myself, especially not when I'm sitting in the same room with alligator meat."

The little boy Bear grabbed one of the baby Alligators and ate him. He didn't leave the head; he didn't leave the tail. And he ate the shadow for dessert.

When he finished chewing and belching, he patted his stomach. "I feel good now. I don't know what I'm gon' tell Miz Alligator when she comes back, but I feel too good to worry about that. I'll worry about it when it's time to worry, and since Miz 'Gator ain't here yet, it ain't time to worry."

The little boy Bear yawned, crawled on the bed, and went to sleep.

Close to nightfall the voice of Miz Alligator woke him up. "Hey, little boy Bear! How can you be minding my children when you sound asleep?"

Little boy Bear said, "My eye went for some sleep, but I'm wide awake!"

Miz Alligator flicked her tail. "Where my children that I left here with you?"

"They here, Miz Alligator." He started pulling the baby Alligators out from under the covers.

> *Here's one, here's another,*
> *Here're two on top of the other,*
> *Here're three piled up together.*

Miz Gator grinned. "You took care of my children very well. Bring me one so I can wash him and feed him his supper."

The little boy Bear carried one to Miz Alligator. He carried another and another and another until he counted six. Then he got scared. Miz Alligator was expecting seven children.

"Bring me the last one," shouted Miz Alligator.

The little boy Bear grabbed one of the babies, smeared some mud over him, and carried him to Miz Alligator. Them was the ugliest children anybody had ever seen, and ugly is ugly. You can't tell one ugly from another ugly. And neither could Miz Alligator. She washed the same one off the second time without knowing it, and the little boy Bear carried it back to the bed.

The next day Miz Alligator left early in the morning. After a while the little boy Bear got hungry. He grabbed another one of the baby alligators and ate it. He thought it tasted like pizza with matzoh balls.

That evening Miz Alligator came home and asked to see her children. There were only five left, so two of them got washed and fed twice.

This went on for five more days, and when the last baby Alligator was eaten, the little boy Bear decided he better go home and see his mama and his sister.

And that's what he did. But he didn't go away again for a long, long time.

Brer Turtle and Brer Mink

Brer Turtle and Brer Mink both lived in the water. Brer Mink knew that Brer Turtle was a smart man, but Brer Mink knew too that Brer Turtle nor anybody else could swim like him. Brer Mink would dive and swim through the water so slick and smooth that the water didn't splash or shudder.

One day Brer Mink was getting out of the creek with a string of fish when along came Brer Turtle.

"What's happening, Brer Mink?"

"Same old same old."

"Them are sho' some good-looking fish you got there. Where'd you get 'em?"

"Where you think? Fish don't grow in trees and neither do they grow out of the ground."

"You got them fish out of the creek?" Brer Turtle asked, amazed.

"Are you going deaf? That's just what I said."

"You don't understand what I'm talking about, Brer Mink. It don't look good for a man who can swim like you to be going in a creek like this. This creek ain't worthy of a swimmer like you. If other folks find out you been swimming in this little dinky creek, they might start thinking you slowing down and can't swim like you used to."

Brer Mink said, "Looks or no looks, there's some good fish in that creek, and I'm going to get me as many of them as I can."

"Well, I'm glad to see you a man what's got a mind of his own. You know, Brer Mink, I always wished I was as good in the water as you are. I done tried to catch fish, but I just can't never seem to catch up to 'em. Maybe if you taught me a few things about swimming, I could learn to catch fish. Don't nobody know as much about water as you do."

Brer Mink swelled up with pride. "What you want to know?"

"Well, let's have a contest and see who can stay underwater the longest. Whoever stays under the longest can have these fish."

Brer Mink chuckled. "I ain't in danger of losing that bet. Let's go, Brer Turtle."

They went down to the creek and waded in.

Brer Turtle jumped back a little bit. "Have mercy! This water is cold! How can you swim in something this cold, Brer Mink? You a better man than I am!"

They got out to where the water was deep. Brer Turtle said, "When I count three, we'll dive under and the contest will start. One, two, three!"

Brer Turtle didn't have his mind on staying underwater any longer than it took him to swim back to the creek bank where the fish were.

He ate every last one of Brer Mink's fish. Then he slid back in the water and swam back out to the middle.

Time he got out there, he came up to the surface kicking and thrashing like he was dangling from the end of somebody's fishing pole. Brer Mink heard all the commotion and came to the top.

Before he can say a word and start bragging, Brer Turtle hollered out, "I should've known you would trick me! I should've known!"

"What're you talking about, Brer Turtle?"

"Don't come asking me what am I talking about! Look over there on the creek bank where you been eating the fish. I should've known you'd trick me!"

Brer Mink looked on the bank, and sho' 'nuf. All his fish were gone. He blinked his eyes once. Twice. Thrice. That's the way they used to say three when I was doing the kinging over in the Land of Aluminum Foil. But that's a story I best keep to myself.

Brer Turtle kept up a steady stream of talk. "While I was down there in the water about to die from lack of breath, you swam to the bank and ate up all the fish which by rights ought to be mine 'cause I was gon' beat you!"

"I didn't eat them fish," Brer Mink said.

"You expect me to believe that? You keep on acting the way you acting, and after a while you'll be worse than Brer Rabbit. You can't expect me to believe you didn't trick me out of them fish when I know good and well that you did."

It made Brer Mink feel proud to be compared to Brer Rabbit, 'cause Brer Rabbit was a mighty man. Brer Mink laughed and acted like he knew more than he was telling.

Brer Turtle kept the talk coming. "I ain't gon' be mad with you, Brer Mink, 'cause that was a mighty good trick you pulled. But you ought to be ashamed of yourself for playing a trick like that on an old man like me."

By this time they had drifted to the bank, and Brer Turtle crawled out and went on down the road. As soon as he was out of sight of Brer Mink, he laughed and laughed until there wasn't any more fun in laughing.

Brer Billy Goat Tricks Brer Wolf

Brer Wolf was going along the road one day and Ol' Man Hungriness was on him. Brer Wolf made up his mind that the first thing he saw, he was going to eat it, regardless.

No sooner was the thought thunk than Brer Wolf rounded a bend and there was Brer Billy Goat standing on top of a rock. This was not one of your little rocks. This rock was as big and broad as a house, and Brer Billy Goat was standing on the top like he owned it and was thinking about turning it into a condominium.

Brer Wolf didn't care about none of that. He charged up the rock to find out what goat meat tasted like.

Brer Billy Goat didn't pay him no mind. He put his head down and went to acting like he was chewing on something. Brer Wolf stopped. He stared at Brer Billy Goat, trying to figure out what he was eating. Brer Billy kept on chewing.

Brer Wolf looked and looked.

Brer Billy Goat chewed and chewed.

Brer Wolf looked close. He didn't see no grass. He didn't see no corn shucks. He didn't see no straw and he didn't see no leaves.

Brer Billy Goat chewed and chewed.

Brer Wolf couldn't figure out to save his life what Brer Billy Goat was eating. Didn't nothing grow on a rock like that. Finally Brer Wolf couldn't stand it anymore.

"How do, Brer Billy Goat? I hope everything is going well with you these days."

Brer Billy Goat nodded and kept on chewing.

"What you eating, Brer Billy Goat? Looks like it tastes mighty good."

Brer Billy Goat looked up. "What does it look like I'm eating? I'm eating this rock."

Brer Wolf said, "Well, I'm powerful hungry myself, but I don't reckon I can eat rock."

"Come on. I'll break you off a chunk with my horns. There's enough here for you, if you hurry."

Brer Wolf shook his head and started backing away. He figured that if Brer Billy Goat could eat rock, he was a tougher man than Brer Wolf was. "Much obliged, Brer Billy Goat. But I got to be moving along."

"Don't go, Brer Wolf. This rock is fresh. Ain't no better rock in these parts."

Brer Wolf didn't even bother to answer but just kept on going. Any creature that could eat rock could eat wolf too.

Of course, Brer Billy Goat wasn't eating that rock. He was just chewing his cud and talking big.

You know something? There're a lot of people like that.

Brer Fox Takes Miz Cricket to Dinner

One of the smallest things on the grassy side of the earth was Miz Cricket. Even though she wasn't big, she could make as big a fuss as anybody. Some of the creatures say she made more fuss than she done good. I don't know about that. I ain't agreeing with it and I ain't disagreeing. The way I look on it, everybody is put on this earth for something, good or bad, and the most we can do is follow our noses if we plan on getting anywhere, and if you don't fall down and get talked about, you can thank all the stars on the underside of the sky.

Miz Cricket lived in the bushes and the high grass, and all she did every day was play on her fife and fiddle. When she got tired of playing on one, she'd play on the other, and that's what she did.

One day King Sun was shining thankful like. Miz Cricket climbed up in the tall grass and fiddled away like the circus was coming to town. Of course, back in them days there wasn't no such thing as a circus, and if there had been, it probably would've been folks who would've been balancing balls on their noses and jumping through fiery hoops. But that's what Miz Cricket's happy fiddling put me in mind of.

Miz Cricket heard somebody coming along the road. She looked real close and it wasn't nobody but Brer Fox.

"Why, hello there, Brer Fox! Where you going?"

Brer Fox stopped and looked around. "Who's that?"

"Ain't nobody in the round world but me. I know I ain't much, but I'm here just the same. Where you going?"

Brer Fox said, "I'm going where I'm going. That's where I'm going, and it wouldn't surprise me if where I was going was to town to get my dinner. I was a rover in my young days and I'm a rover now."

"I know what you mean, Brer Fox. We all go the way we're pushed by mind or hand, and it don't take much of a shove to send us the way we're going. I used to be a rover myself, but I've settled down and don't do nothing but have my own fun in my own way and time. But listening to you has got me to thinking about having my dinner in town."

"How you going to get there?"

"What you mean? I got legs and feet, and I caught the jumping habit from Cousin Brown Grasshopper. He's the kind what crawls a little, walks a little, flies a little, and hops a little. What time will you get to town?"

Brer Fox thought for a minute and did some counting on his fingers. "It'll take me a good two hours. My appetite will get there first but I won't be far behind."

Miz Cricket was astonished. She held up all her hands and feet and did some counting. "Two hours!" she exclaimed. "By the time you get there, Brer Fox, I'll be belching and picking my teeth and ready to take my after-dinner nap."

Brer Fox laughed. "If you beat me to town by so much as ten seconds, I'll buy your dinner and you can order from the menu that don't have no prices on it. But if I beat you, you'll have to pay for my dinner and I'm gon' tell you now: I'm powerful hungry."

"Brer Fox! It's a deal!"

Brer Fox grinned and started off down the road.

Just as Brer Fox made his start, Miz Cricket made hers. She took a flying jump and landed in Brer Fox's bushy tail, where she made herself comfortable and went to sleep.

Brer Fox had been going down the road about an hour when he met up with Brer Rabbit. They howdied and inquired about each other's family, and then Brer Fox told Brer Rabbit about the race he was having with Miz Cricket.

Brer Rabbit saw Miz Cricket nestled in Brer Fox's tail, and she gave him a big wink. He smole a smile and rolled his eyeballs. Brer Fox wanted to know what was wrong with him.

"Well, I was just thinking about how you'd feel if you knew that Miz Cricket was winning the race," said Brer Rabbit. "She passed me on the road about fifteen minutes ago. What have you been doing all this time? You must've fallen asleep and didn't know it."

"I been coming full tilt the whole time."

"If that's so, Miz Cricket got a whole lot of talent for covering ground. She probably in town now, waiting for you."

Brer Fox took off running, but as fast as he went, that was how fast Miz Cricket went.

When Brer Rabbit saw Brer Fox kicking up dust and moving down the road, he laughed so hard that he fell over in a ditch. "I'm mighty glad I met my old friend, 'cause now I know that all the fools ain't dead—and long may they live, 'cause it gives me something to do. Don't nothing keep me fat and sassy as good as a fool."

About forty-five minutes later Brer Fox got to the gate of the town. Back in them days all the towns had walls around them, and the only way in and out was through a gate. That's an idea that ought to be revived. I know a whole bunch of folks ought to be kept outside the gate.

When Brer Fox got to the gate, Miz Cricket took a flying jump and landed on top of the wall. Brer Fox knocked on the gate.

Miz Cricket yelled down from the top of the wall, "Hey, Brer Fox! Where you been? You must've stopped and had

a snack somewhere. I done ate my dinner already, but that was so long ago, I believe I could eat another one."

Brer Fox looked up and couldn't believe his eyes. "How in the wide world did you get here so quick?"

Miz Cricket said, "You know how I travel—with a hop, skip, and a jump. Well, I hopped and skipped and jumped a little quicker this time. I run into Brer Rabbit and he wanted to stop and talk, but I know that the only way to get where you going is to go on and get there. I reckon you must've run into Brer Rabbit too and let him get you tied up in his tongue."

Brer Porcupine was the gatekeeper, and he opened it. Brer Fox took Miz Cricket to dinner at the best restaurant in town. I think it was the Chez Stomachache. Then again it might've been the House of Grease and Good Times.

Brer Fox didn't know how somebody so little could eat so much. She had a great big porterhouse steak, baked potato, broccoli with French dressing, and washed it all down with a seventy-five-dollar bottle of wine. For dessert she had French vanilla ice cream with fresh strawberries. She finished it all off with a pot of black coffee. Luckily Brer Fox never left home without his American Express card, 'cause he sho' needed it that night.

Miz Cricket Makes the Creatures Run

Miz Cricket had almost as much sense as Brer Rabbit. Back in them times the big creatures had the strength, but the little ones had the sense.

One summer day the creatures were laying out in the meadow getting suntans. Don't ask me how come the creatures wanted tans. I ain't figured out how come white folks work so hard to get tans. Deep down I think they want to look as good as us black folks do, 'cause they sho' work overtime at it. I reckon the creatures wanted to look black too.

There they were out there in the meadow slapping suntan lotion on each other and turning this way and that way to make sure their tans were even all over, and that's what caused all the trouble.

What's true for folks was true for the creatures. When folks ain't got much to do and ain't got much more to talk about, somebody will start in bragging, and trouble ain't far behind. Brer Fox was the one what started this time.

"I was just lying here thinking that I'm the swiftest one of anybody here."

Brer Elephant winked one of his tiny eyes, flung his trunk in the air, and whispered—of course, when Brer Elephant whispered, folks a mile away could hear it—"I got the most strength!"

King Lion was there and he shook his mane and showed his teeth. "Don't forget! I'm the King of all you creatures."

Brer Tiger stretched himself and yawned. "I'm the prettiest and the most vigorous."

The bragging went on this way until all the creatures had declared that he was the most something or other. The only one that hadn't bragged was Miz Cricket, and didn't nobody expect her to do no bragging, 'cause as far as they were concerned, she didn't have nothing to brag about.

So everybody was astonished when Miz Cricket said, "I can make all of you run your heads off, all of you from Brer Elephant on down."

The creatures thought that was the funniest thing they'd heard since somebody played them a record called *Luciano Pavarotti Sings the Blues.*

Brer Fox said, "I hear you talking, Miss Cricket, but what I want to know is, how you gon' do it?"

"Don't worry about it. You'll hear from me. That you will."

The creatures thought that was the second funniest thing they'd ever heard and they took to laughing some more.

They were laughing so hard, they didn't notice that Brer Rabbit wasn't laughing at all. He knew Miz Cricket was powerful in the mind, and he wanted to know what she was up to. It just so happened that Miz Cricket wanted to exchange a few syllables with Brer Rabbit, 'cause she needed some help.

Brer Rabbit and Miz Cricket sneaked off where they could talk.

"You got a big job on your hands," said Brer Rabbit.

"I know, and I can't do it if I don't get your help."

Brer Rabbit twisted his mustache and looked thoughtful. "Well, I don't know, Miz Cricket. All the creatures been after me so fierce lately that I done had to lay low. But what's on your mind?"

Miz Cricket told Brer Rabbit what she was planning and Brer Rabbit laughed. "If that's all you want me to do, Miz Cricket, I'm your man!"

The next day Miz Cricket and Brer Rabbit went back to the meadow where they knew they'd find all the creatures. The first one they saw was Brer Elephant.

"I got some bad news," Brer Rabbit told him.

"What's the trouble?"

"A big wind came up last night and blew a tree down on Miz Cricket and broke one of her legs. She can't get to the hospital to get it attended to. I was wondering if you'd be so kind as to carry her there."

Brer Elephant said he'd be glad to. He knelt down and Brer Rabbit put Miz Cricket on his back. But Miz Cricket didn't stay on Brer Elephant's back. She crawled up to his neck and down into his ear.

As soon as she was in his ear, she started fluttering her wings. Brer Elephant thought a big wind was blowing through the trees. Miz Cricket fluttered her wings faster. It sounded like a storm was coming, and Brer Elephant took off running through the woods. He plunged through the bushes and knocked over trees, but the storm kept getting louder and louder. It was good thing Miz Cricket was inside his ear or she would've been knocked off and trampled on.

Miz Cricket took out her fife and started playing on it. She played kind of low to begin with and then got louder and louder. The louder she played, the more scared Brer Elephant got, and the more scared he got, the more he ran. He ran round and round in circles, his trunk flapping in the air, and pretty soon he ran back to the meadow.

"Where you going?" King Lion asked him, jumping up.

Brer Elephant stopped, almost out of breath. "I got a singing and whistling in my ears and I don't know where it's coming from. Can't you hear it?"

The creatures listened and they heard it.

King Lion said, "Seems to me, Brer Elephant, that that whistling sound means that you about to boil over, and if that's what you going to do, I believe I want to be way away from here."

While King Lion was saying all that, Miz Cricket took a flying jump out of Brer Elephant's ear and landed right smack dab in King Lion's ear.

Brer Elephant said, "Wait a minute! I don't hear it no more." He listened. "Sho' 'nuf. The whistling done stopped." He smiled. "I'm cured. I don't know which one of you is a doctor, but I thank you for curing me."

By this time Miz Cricket had gotten comfortable in King Lion's ear and took out her fife and started playing.

King Lion cocked his head to one side and listened. "You might not hear it no more, Brer Elephant, but I can still hear it. I think I done caught what you was just cured of."

Miz Cricket played louder and King Lion started getting fidgety, like there was someplace he had to go but he don't know where it is. He waved his tail and shook his mane. Miz Cricket played louder and fluttered her wings.

"I hear the wind blowing," said King Lion. "I got to go home and see after my family." He took off and he ran and he ran trying to get away from all the noise in his ear. He ran to where he didn't know and come back to where he did know which is where he'd started from but he didn't know that.

"What y'all chasing me for?" he asked the other creatures. "I left y'all back yonder where I came from."

"We ain't moved out of our tracks," Brer Elephant said.

"You ran away and left us here and now you come back," added Brer Tiger. "What's the matter with you?"

"I got a whistling in my head and can't get away from it. I don't know what I'm going to do."

"Ain't nothing you can do except do like I did and stand it as best you can," Brer Elephant offered.

Brer Tiger said, "I hear it and it sounds like you gon' boil over any minute. I know I don't want to be here when you do."

While Brer Tiger was saying that, Miz Cricket took a flying leap out of King Lion's ear and landed right smack dab in Brer Tiger's. Soon as she got comfortable, she began playing on her fife and flapping her wings. Brer Tiger started getting fidgety and moving around.

"Has the disease got you now?" Brer Elephant wanted to know.

Brer Tiger didn't wait around to answer, 'cause he was galloping across the meadow like a racehorse.

Brer Rabbit walked up to the creatures, chuckling. "Miz Cricket said she was going to make y'all run, and that's just what she done. If you just wait here, Miz Cricket will bring Brer Tiger back in a few minutes."

Sure enough it wasn't long before Brer Tiger came back with his tongue dragging on the ground. Miz Cricket jumped out of Brer Tiger's ear and bowed real low to all the gentlemen.

"Howdy do, everybody."

But the creatures didn't want any "howdy-doing" with Miz Cricket after that.

It serves 'em right for laying out there slapping suntan oil on themselves and trying to get tans. If the Lord had wanted them to be as pretty as black folks, they would've been born black. But they wasn't and they should've been content with what the Lord blessed 'em with.

———————————

The Story of the Doodang

I know the first thing you want to know is, what is a Doodang? Well, I can't tell you, 'cause I ain't never seen one. However I have seen them what say they heard tell of them who had seen him.

The way I heard it was that the Doodang lived in the mud flats down on the river. Didn't nobody know exactly what kind of creature he was. He had a long tail like an alligator, a great big body, four short legs, two short ears, and a head that was uglier than a rhinoceros's. His mouth went from the end of his nose to his shoulder blades, and his teeth were big enough and long enough and sharp enough to bite off the left hind leg of a bull elephant.

The Doodang could live in the water and he could live on dry land, but his favorite place was the mud flats. He could sit on the mud flats, reach out in the water, and catch a fish, or he could reach up in the bushes and catch a bird.

To you and me it might seem that the Doodang had the best of both worlds, dry and wet, but that ain't the way it seemed to the Doodang.

He got dissatisfied and started wanting things he didn't have. What he had didn't satisfy him and he started worrying. His worrying turned to growling and groaning all through the day and all through the night.

His groaning and growling kept all the creatures, fur and feather, wing and claw, wide awake for miles around.

After a week without any good sleep Brer Rabbit had had quite enough. He went down to the river to see the Doodang.

"What is the matter with you?" Brer Rabbit said right

off. He didn't waste no time with howdy-dos and all like that, and to tell the truth Brer Rabbit didn't phrase the question as politely as I did.

You would think that a creature as big as the Doodang would've had a deep bass voice. Truth is his voice was high pitched, and when he talked it sounded like he was whining. "I want to swim in the water like the fish do."

Brer Rabbit shivered. "You make my blood run cold when you talk about swimming in the water. The Lord put the water on earth so we'd have something to make Kool-Aid out of, but if you want to swim, swim on dry land! Swim on dry land!"

The Doodang talked so loud that the fish heard him. Like everybody else they hadn't been able to get any sleep, and they were so tired they had started biting at fishing worms. They held a meeting out there in the river.

"Did you hear that fool Doodang say he wants to swim like we do?" said Brer Catfish.

"I wouldn't mind teaching him how to swim," said Brer Mackerel, "but he ain't got no scales and fins."

"That's it!" said Miz Goldfish.

"What's it?" all the other fish wanted to know.

"Why don't we lend him one scale and one fin apiece?"

The fish agreed that that was the thing to do, and no sooner said than done.

They swam over and told the Doodang what they were going to do. He was so happy that he gave a loud howl and rolled over in the water.

The fish surrounded him and each one took a scale and a fin and put it on the Doodang. When they got through, the Doodang took a deep breath and plunged into the water.

He skeeted about in the water, waving his tail from side to side. He swam up the river and down the river and went back and forth across the river. He swam on the top-side of the water and underneath the water. He had a good time being a fish—for about an hour or so. Then he got tired and bored and started walking out of the water.

"Hey!" the fish yelled out. "Where you going?"

"It's not fun being a fish," said the Doodang.

"Then give us back our fins and scales!"

The fish were so mad they were ready to fight, so the Doodang gave them back their fins and scales and crawled onto the mud flats to take a nap.

He hadn't been asleep long when a big noise woke him. He looked up and the blue sky was black with birds, big ones and little ones. They were coming to roost in the trees on the island in the middle of the river.

The birds had scarcely gotten settled before the Doo-dang started howling and growling and carrying on like he had eaten too many hot dogs.

The King-Bird flew over to the mud flat. "What is wrong with you?" he screamed at the Doodang.

The Doodang rolled over on his back and started howl-ing louder.

"WHAT IS WRONG WITH YOU?"

The Doodang just lay there and howled and howled. Finally he raised his head and said, "I want to fly."

"You doofus Doodang! You can't fly. You too big to fly!" the King-Bird yelled.

"If I had some feathers, I bet I could fly. I bet I could fly as good as you—if I had some feathers."

The King-Bird flew back to the island and held a meet-ing with all the birds.

"Listen up, everybody!" said the King-Bird. "We got to get us some sleep. Ain't no two ways about it. The Doodang said if he had some feathers he could fly, and if he's flying, he ain't hollering, and if he ain't hollering, we can get some sleep. I say each of us lend him a feather."

The King-Bird hadn't finished his speech before the birds started taking off feathers. They took 'em to the Doodang and put them on him.

The Doodang looked at his new feathers and he was as

proud as a little boy who's been playing in the mud. "Where should I fly to?" he wanted to know.

Brer Buzzard said, "There's another island about a mile down the river that ain't got nothing but dead trees on it. Why don't you see if you can fly down there?"

The Doodang got a running start, jumped up in the air, and started moving his wings. Wouldn't nobody ever say that the Doodang looked pretty flying, but he stayed in the air, and that was the main thing.

In a little while he landed with a splash in the water next to the island. He was spluttering around in the water when Brer Buzzard said, "I don't want my feather getting all wet. Won't be good for flying then." He swooped down and grabbed his feather off the Doodang.

Soon as he did that, the other birds swooped down and took their feathers back. And then they flew away.

There the Doodang was on the island with the dead trees and no way to get back to the mud flats.

All the creatures went to sleep that night and they slept that night, all the next day, the next night, and half of the following day.

On the day after that Brer Rabbit happened to run into Brer Buzzard. "Say, Brer Buzzard, what happened to the Doodang?"

Brer Buzzard pointed down the river to the island where the dead trees were. "You see my family sitting in them dead trees?"

Brer Rabbit nodded.

"That's where the Doodang is. If you'll get me a bag, Brer Rabbit, I'll bring you his bones."

Brer Rabbit laughed and laughed and laughed.

Brer Deer and King Sun's Daughter

One of the problems with telling tales like these is that it ain't always easy to get the story fixed in the time it's supposed to be in. That's because there're so many different kinds of time.

There's daytime and nighttime, bedtime and mealtime. There's sometime, any ol' time, and no time. There's high time, fly time, good times, bad times, and the wrong time, not to mention a long time and time to go. All the different kinds of time are enough to give a body a headache and turn him white. I've been trying to count up all the different times, and my calculator can't count that high. There's new time and old time, cold time and due time, and then there's once upon a time.

Some folks say that this story happened "once upon a time," but I ain't sure about that. The once-upon-a-time stories got people in them, but this story took place before then. So I can't start it off with "Once upon a time." Let me think a minute.

All right. I got it.

Way back before there was a time, Brer Deer fell in love with King Sun's daughter. Back in the time what I'm talking about, King Sun wasn't like he is now. He was as different then as them times are from these times. For one thing he was a lot closer to the earth then. For another he didn't go off and hide at night like he does now. King Sun was a lot more neighborly in them days than he is now, when he don't talk to nobody.

Back in them times he lived so close that he used to send one of his servants down to the spring for drinking water. Three times a day he'd climb down with a bucket in his hand and climb back up with the bucket on his head.

All the creatures knew King Sun had a pretty daughter, but none of 'em had ever seen her. That didn't matter to Brer Deer. He made up his mind that he was going to marry her. The only problem was that he had to find a way to ask her.

He was sitting beside the road trying to figure out a plan when along came Brer Rabbit.

"Well, Brer Deer. How is your copperosity segashuating?"

"My copperosity is segashuating just fine, Brer Rabbit, but I got trouble in my mind and I can't get it out."

"I'm sorry to hear that." Brer Rabbit sat down looking like he knew all there was to be known. "When I was a little rabbit, I heard the old folks say that a light heart make for a long life. They knew what they was talking about, 'cause I been here longer than anybody."

Brer Deer sighed. He blinked his eyes real fast to keep the tears in 'em from falling out. "I know you telling me the truth, Brer Rabbit, but I can't help myself. I am what I am and I can't be no ammer. I feel more like crying than eating, and I seem to get angry for no reason. Just a little while ago Mr. Benjamin Ram told me howdy, and for no reason I ran at him and butted him with my horns. Now, I know that wasn't the right thing to do, but I couldn't help myself."

Brer Rabbit got up and put a little distance between himself and Brer Deer. "Now that you mention it, them horns of yours have always made me a little nervous."

"I ain't gon' do *you* no harm, Brer Rabbit. We been knowing each other a long time, and I'm glad you come by. If I don't tell my troubles to somebody, I'm going to bust wide open."

Brer Rabbit sat down close to Brer Deer again. "What's your trouble?"

"I'm in love with King Sun's daughter. I don't know how it happened, but it did. I ain't never talked to her. I ain't never laid eyes on her, but I'm in love with her just the same. You can laugh at me if you want to, but truth is truth."

Brer Rabbit didn't laugh. He felt sorry for Brer Deer. Falling in love was hard on the appetite and on your sleep. I don't want to have nothing to do with something that makes me leave food on my plate and lie in bed at night tossing and turning. Brer Rabbit knew that the best cure for falling in love was getting married, so he decided to help Brer Deer out of his misery.

Brer Deer perked up. "If you help me through this, I'll be your friend forever."

Brer Rabbit shook his head. "Having a friend forever would make me kind of nervous. To be truthful I been feeling kind of bored the past few weeks, so this will give me something to occupy my mind." Brer Rabbit got up and brushed the dirt off his pants. "I hope to have some good news for you the next time we meet in the big road."

Brer Rabbit went on down the road and Brer Deer found him a cool spot in the woods and got the first sleep he'd had in weeks.

Brer Rabbit went to the spring where King Sun's servant came to get water. He had to carry a lot of water too. The more water King Sun drank, the more he wanted, so the servant was carrying water almost all day every day.

Brer Rabbit got to the spring and it was just as clear as glass. He leaned over, looked in, and saw himself. "Whoever you are, you as pretty as sin." He laughed.

Down at the bottom of the spring was Ol' Man Spring Lizard. He was taking his morning nap and woke up when he heard somebody talking. He looked up to see Brer Rabbit looking at himself in the water.

"Maybe you ain't as good looking as you think you are," the Spring Lizard hollered up.

"I ain't never had my reflection talk back at me before," Brer Rabbit said.

Mr. Spring Lizard swam from under the green moss and came to the top. He asked Brer Rabbit what he was up to.

Brer Rabbit told him about Brer Deer being in love with King Sun's daughter.

"I seen her once. A few months back she came down here to the spring. She's got an Afro that's light and fluffy like clouds and eyes that shine like love."

"Do tell!" said Brer Rabbit. "Well, I got to figure out how to get word to her that Brer Deer wants to marry her."

"That's easy."

"Talk to me, Mr. Spring Lizard."

"When the servant comes from King Sun's house, he has to let down a ladder. When he does, you can just slip up it."

Brer Rabbit wasn't too sure he wanted to met with King Sun face to face. "I'm a homebody, you know, and don't like going off on long trips."

"Well, if Brer Deer will write a note, I'll get in the bucket and take it up."

"That's a good idea. Brer Deer can't write, but I can. I be back in a little while."

Brer Rabbit went home, wrote the note, and brought it back. "Don't let this note get wet."

Mr. Spring Lizard acted disgusted. "How can the note get wet when I'll have it in my pocket? You land creatures got the wrong idea about water. What's wet to you ain't wet to us, excepting on rainy days."

Before long King Sun's servant let down the ladder and came to the spring with his bucket. He dropped the bucket in and filled it with water. The Spring Lizard swam in at the last minute and hid down at the bottom. The servant took the bucket, climbed back up the ladder, and pulled it up after him. Then he went along the path to King Sun's house.

He brought the bucket of water to King Sun, who grabbed his dipper and drank and drank until it looked like his fire might go out. But he had his fill before that happened and he went on in the back to take a nap.

Soon as he was gone, Mr. Spring Lizard leaped out of the bucket, put the note on the table, and jumped back in.

In a little while King Sun's daughter came bouncing in the room to get herself a drink of water and saw the note. She picked it up.

"Daddy! Daddy! Here's a letter for you."

King Sun came in the room, pulled his fingers through his beard, put on his glasses, and read the note, "Well, well, well. I ain't never heard of such impudence."

"What does it say, Daddy?"

"Dear King Sun: I would be most honored and proud if you would permit me to be the one to marry your daughter. I will take care of her better than anybody. If you grant my request, it will make me very happy. (Signed) Brer Deer."

King Sun's daughter got all red in the face and she got mad and she got glad and she didn't know what to think. That was the sign that she had fallen in love.

King Sun got out his pen and some writing paper and wrote a letter back to Brer Deer. *If the one who wrote the letter will send me a bag of gold, he can marry my daughter. (Signed) King Sun.* He gave the letter to his daughter and she put it on the table where she'd found the other one.

When they left the room, Mr. Spring Lizard jumped out of the bucket, got the letter, and jumped back in without making a splash.

A little while later the servant came in, took the bucket, let down the ladder, and went to the spring. Mr. Spring Lizard jumped into the water and waited for Brer Rabbit.

Brer Rabbit had been hiding in the bushes, waiting, and as soon as the servant left, he went to the spring, got the letter from Mr. Spring Lizard, and went directly to Brer Deer and read it to him.

In no time at all Brer Deer had gathered up a bag of gold. Don't come asking me where he got the gold. That information must not have been important, 'cause it wasn't in the story when the story was handed to me, and I'm too tired to put it in today.

Brer Deer left the bag of gold at the spring and waited. Wasn't long before he saw the ladder being let down, but it wasn't the servant who walked down. It was King Sun's daughter herself. She was coming to see what kind of man Brer Deer was.

Brer Deer looked at her and was glad that he had listened to his heart, even though what his heart had been saying hadn't made no sense to his brain. King Sun's daughter had an Afro that curved around her head like a shining halo. Her skin was a deep brown like earth that had just been turned over by a plow. Her eyes glistened like they were the place where joy had been born.

Brer Deer got up his courage and stepped out from hiding, so King Sun's daughter could see him. She looked at him and he looked at her, and it was over for both of 'em. And from what I understand, they were happy with one another, except on Sundays, when Brer Deer didn't pay her no attention 'cause he was watching football on TV.

———————————

Teenchy-Tiny Duck's Magical Satchel

Once there lived a man and a woman, and they were very poor. They didn't have any money. They didn't have a farm. They didn't even have a garden patch.

All they had in the whole world was a little puddle duck who walked around all day singing the hungry song: "Quack! Quack! Give me a piece of bread!" It wouldn't have taken much to feed her because she was so tiny, which was why folks called her Teenchy-Tiny Duck.

One day she was paddling in the river when she found a money purse filled with gold. As soon as she saw what it was, she started quacking: "Somebody lost their pretty money! Pretty money! Pretty money! Who lost their pretty money?"

Just about the same time a rich man came walking along. He had a walking stick in his hand, and every few steps he stopped and made some marks in the dirt, trying to add up all the money he had. He heard Teenchy-Tiny Duck making a lot of racket, and his eye lit on the money purse.

"That's mine! That's mine! I lost it and came back to look for it." He picked up the money purse and dropped it in his satchel.

Teenchy-Tiny got mad! "That rascal just came and took all the gold I found and didn't even give me none for finding it!"

She waddled home and told the folks what had happened. The poor man was so mad that he started pulling his hair out. "Get out of my house!" he yelled at Teenchy-Tiny Duck. "Get out and don't come back until you get the gold what that rich man took!"

Teenchy-Tiny didn't know what to do. She went back to the river and sat on the bank and started crying.

Well, it just so happened that Brer Rabbit was laying over in the weeds trying to figure out how come he was so smart, and he heard Teenchy-Tiny crying. "What's the matter, little puddle-duck?" he asked her.

She told him about finding the gold and the rich man taking it from her. Brer Rabbit cried with one eye and winked the other. "Well, go after him and get the gold back."

"How am I going to do that?" Teenchy-Tiny wanted to know.

"There's always a way, if not two."

Teenchy-Tiny started off down the road after the man, waddling and quacking as fast as she could. "I want my pretty money! I want my pretty money!"

After a while she came upon Brer Fox.

"Where you going?" he wanted to know.

She told him.

"What you gon' do when you find that rich man?"

"I'm gon' get my money and take it back home."

"You want me to go with you?" asked Brer Fox.

"Wouldn't nothing suit me better."

"Well, I have to hide."

Teenchy-Tiny had brought a satchel with her to carry the gold in when she got it back. "Get in my satchel."

"It ain't big enough," said Brer Fox.

"This here is a stretching satchel."

Brer Fox jumped in.

Not long after that Teenchy-Tiny met Brer Wolf.

"Where you going?" he wanted to know.

She told him.

"Maybe I can help you, but I'm tired and I can't go too far."

"Get in my satchel."

"It ain't big enough," Brer Wolf said.

"This here is a stretching satchel. Jump in."

Brer Wolf jumped in and Teenchy-Tiny Duck went on down the road.

The next somebody she ran into was Uncle Ladder, who was taking his noonday rest by the side of a tree. He wanted to know where Teenchy-Tiny was going.

She told him.

Uncle Ladder felt sorry for her. "You think I could help you out?"

"No doubt about it."

"Well, I be glad to, but I can't walk fast as you."

"Don't need to. Just get in my satchel and I'll carry you."

Uncle Ladder got in the satchel and off Teenchy-Tiny went down the road, quacking and squawking about getting her pretty money back.

The road curved and Teenchy-Tiny Duck found herself next to the best friend she'd ever had, Grandpappy River. He stopped running. "What's the matter? When I saw you this morning, you were happy. Now you look like you in bad trouble. How can I help you? I'd go along with you if I had legs."

"Just get in the satchel, Grandpappy."

Grandpappy River got in the satchel and didn't drown nobody. Teenchy-Tiny went on down the road. "I want my money! I want my money!"

After a while she came to a big beehive. Ol' Man Drone was sunning himself and he started laughing at the little duck toting a satchel that was seventy-eleven times bigger than she was. But when him and all the Bees saw how sorrowful Teenchy-Tiny was looking, they asked her what was wrong.

She told them all about her troubles and it seemed like the more she talked, the bigger her troubles got.

The Bees said they'd be proud to go with her.

"Get in the satchel, but don't be stinging nobody."

The Bees got in the satchel and kept their stingers to themselves.

Teenchy-Tiny went on down the road, and late over in the evening she came to the rich man's house. She went up to the gate. "Hey, stupid rich man! You bring me my money!"

The rich man laughed and told one of his servants, "Go get that duck. I believe I'll have her for supper tomorrow."

The servant grabbed Teenchy-Tiny and threw her and the satchel in the henhouse.

Soon as she was inside, the chickens started pecking and beating on Teenchy-Tiny something awful.

Teenchy-Tiny wasn't in no mood for nothing but her money, so she opened up the satchel. "Brer Fox!"

Brer Fox jumped out, saw all those chickens, and knew he was in paradise. Wasn't long before there was nothing but silence in that henhouse.

Next morning when the servant came to the henhouse, there wasn't a chicken there. However there were a whole lot of chicken feathers.

The servant couldn't believe his eyes, and while he was standing in the door wondering what to do, Teenchy-Tiny picked up her satchel and marched out, shouting, "I want my money! I want my money!"

When the servant told the rich man and his wife what had happened, the wife said, "That ain't no duck. That's a witch. You better give her that money!"

The rich man just laughed.

All day long Teenchy-Tiny stood outside the house, shouting, "I want my money! I want my money!"

Night came, as night is prone to do, and the rich man told the servant, "Put that duck in the stable with the mules and the horses. They'll take care of her."

The servant put Teenchy-Tiny and her satchel in the stable.

Teenchy-Tiny was scared that the horses and mules might step on her during the night. She opened up the satchel. "Brer Wolf!"

Brer Wolf leaped out, saw all the horses and mules, and thought he was in paradise. The next morning when the farmhands came down to the stable to hitch up the horses and the mules, every last one of 'em was stretched out cold.

When they told the rich man what had happened, his wife started crying. "Give that duck her gold! If you don't, it's gon' be the end of us!"

The rich man was mad now. He told his servant, "Throw that duck in the well!"

The servant threw Teenchy-Tiny in the well. Teenchy-Tiny squawked and yelled until Uncle Ladder heard her. He got out of the satchel and stretched himself, 'cause a satchel ain't a comfortable place for a ladder. He managed to make his way over to the well and let himself down so that Teenchy-Tiny Duck could climb out.

That's what she did, and wasn't but one thing on her mind. "I want my pretty money! Give my my pretty money!"

The rich man was sho' 'nuf mad now. He told his cook, "Get the oven heated up!"

All while the oven was getting red hot, Teenchy-Tiny

was yelling, "I want my money! Give me my pretty money!"

The rich man told his servant, "Throw that duck in the oven!"

The servant grabbed Teenchy-Tiny and threw her in the oven.

"Grandpappy River!" hollered Teenchy-Tiny.

Grandpappy River came pouring out of the satchel and headed straight for the oven and drowned the fire. Teenchy-Tiny came marching out of the oven, hollering, "Where's my pretty money? I want my money!"

The rich man's wife begged and begged, but the rich man wasn't listening. "I'll take care of that duck myself."

Late that night the rich man sneaked out in the yard. Teenchy-Tiny was hollering so loud for her money that she wouldn't had heard the man if he'd driven up in a fire engine with the siren on. The first thing she knew, the rich man was beating her with his walking stick. He was about to beat her into soup or pâté, depending on your preference, when Teenchy-Tiny yelled, "Bees!"

The Bees came swarming out of the satchel. The way they stung that rich man was enough to make you smile or cry, depending on which way your mind leans. The rich man couldn't run fast enough to get that money. He gave it to Teenchy-Tiny Duck and told her to please leave him alone.

Everybody thanked Teenchy-Tiny for the fun adventure and got in the magical satchel so she could take them back where she'd found them. Brer Wolf and Brer Fox didn't like the way the Bees were buzzing and said they'd get home on their own. Teenchy-Tiny carried the Bees back to the hive, the Ladder to the tree, and Grandpappy River to his bed.

Then, Teenchy-Tiny went home and gave the gold to her master and mistress, and after that Teenchy-Tiny had plenty to eat and she got right fat and plump.

But folks called her Teenchy-Tiny just the same.

Julius Lester is the critically acclaimed author of books for both children and adults. His first two collections of Uncle Remus stories, *The Tales of Uncle Remus: The Adventures of Brer Rabbit* and *More Tales of Uncle Remus: Further Adventures of Brer Rabbit, His Friends, Enemies, and Others,* have won numerous awards. Both were ALA Notable Books, Coretta Scott King Honor Books, and *Booklist* Editors' Choices. Other books for Dial include *To Be a Slave,* a Newbery Medal Honor Book; *Long Journey Home: Stories from Black History,* a National Book Award finalist; *This Strange New Feeling;* and *The Knee-High Man and Other Tales,* an ALA Notable Book, *School Library Journal* Best Book of the Year, and Lewis Carroll Shelf Award Winner. His adult books include *Do Lord Remember Me,* a *New York Times* Notable Book, and *Lovesong: Becoming a Jew,* a National Jewish Book Award finalist.

Mr. Lester was born in St. Louis and grew up in Kansas City, Kansas, and Nashville, Tennessee, where he received his Bachelor of Arts from Fisk University. He is married and the father of four children. He lives in Amherst and teaches at the University of Massachusetts.

Jerry Pinkney, a 1989 Caldecott Honor Book artist, is the only illustrator ever to have won the Coretta Scott King Award three times. He illustrated *The Patchwork Quilt* (Dial) by Valerie Flournoy, which in addition to the Coretta Scott King Award also won the Christopher Award and was an IRA-CBC Children's Choice, an ALA Notable Book, and a Reading Rainbow Selection. Mr. Pinkney's recent work for Dial includes illustrations for *The Talking Eggs* by Robert D. San Souci and *Rabbit Makes a Monkey of Lion* by Verna Aardema, which won First Place in the 1989 New York Book Show. His artwork has been shown at the Bologna Book Fair, the AIGA Book Show, the Society of Illustrators Annual Show, and in museums around the country.

Mr. Pinkney is Associate Professor of Art at the University of Delaware. He and his wife Gloria are the parents of four children. They live in Croton-on-Hudson, New York.